TITLE

Blotting on moon

Chapter 1

MAYA

At whatever point I shut my eyes there was one second I envisioned. A home, a family. It was all I needed. As the vagrant of the pack, all I needed was some place to have a place. At the point when the caution went off at 12 PM I grinned. "Glad Birthday..." I murmured to myself and my wolf.

Cheerful birthday, Maya, my wolf, Aspen, answered in my mind.

I shut my eyes and moved back finished, tumbling to rest for an additional couple of hours, knowing today I was 21 and presently ready to observe a mate and the home I had been yearning for.

I got up at six and got wearing my straightforward garments for the day of work in front of me. In the Aurora Pack, everybody was relied upon to do their part. Since this was a cultivating local area, the greater part of us worked in the fields, planting and gathering and really focusing on our harvests and animals. I was one of the unfortunate pack individuals who had the joy of working in the fields. We had 900 sections of land in no place where we raised steers, chickens, and pigs for meat just as cultivating a large portion of the land for food. Our pack provided the nourishment for a large portion of the encompassing packs, procuring us insurance and help when we wanted it. Not that we could possibly do. No one at any point assaulted Aurora. We were a quiet pack that never led to any issues and packs didn't dare trouble us. They thought we were odd and didn't have any desire to chance losing their food supply.

I left my room in the primary packhouse and to the kitchen for breakfast.

"Cheerful morning, Maya," Luna Haven grinned energetically as she gave me a plate.

"Glad morning, Luna," I answered happily and a slight bow of the head. I strolled to a table and plunked somewhere around myself. There were just two others in the pack that really focused on me and they didn't appear to be here yet.

"Hello, Maya!" Gavin hollered as he strolled across the eating lobby to me. He plunked down happily, "Glad birthday."

"Much obliged," I answered with a smile prior to glancing around. "Where's Penelope?"

He feigned exacerbation, "Fixing her hair or her cosmetics or something like that."

I laughed when I saw Penelope stroll up behind him with a glare prior to smacking his head. Gavin and Penelope were twins and were my closest companions. My main companions, assuming we were being honest.

"Glad birthday, Maya," she winked as she sat next to her sibling. She inclined in, "Additionally, did any other individual notification now particularly high our Luna appears to be earlier today?" She emulated the Luna's bow and "cheerful morning", procuring a giggle from most of us.

"She's forever been a tad of a hippy however," I answered.

"Better believe it however she's additional natural earlier today," Gavin laughed.

Penelope checked out the feasting corridor, "So would we say we are taking wagers on who your mate is?"

I giggled as Gavin and Penelope started highlighting the most sweltering wolves in the pack, making surmises about assuming that they were adequate for me. I grinned at my companions, happy I had them.

My folks passed on when I was only a little guy, letting me be. I had been taken in by the pack and brought up in the packhouse, not actually having a family. Despite the fact that I was Gamma conceived, I wasn't viewed as much as a vagrant. No one truly minded, until I met Penelope and Gavin.

"We should take off," Penelope said prior to remaining from the table.

I moaned, "One more day in the fields."

Penelope and Gavin, as Beta-conceived wolves, might have had their pick of occupations in the pack. However, they decided to work in the fields with me, guaranteeing they would have rather not be caught inside morning, noon and night.

We remained outside as we accepted our tasks for the afternoon. We buckled down the entire morning, at last halting at noon for a break. We plunked down in the feasting corridor again and had our lunch discreetly, grimy and tired from the difficult work.

"Gavin, Penelope, mother needs you higher up," their more established sibling Chase said as he approached the table.

Gavin let out a moan, whining about getting up as he remained from the table. I gazed toward Chase happily. He looked very much like his more youthful kin, attractive and solid from long periods of preparing as a Beta. He didn't actually give a lot of consideration to me, similar to the remainder of the pack, however he was dependably kind. He peered down with a little grin, "Hello Maya… " he followed off as our eyes met.

Aspen was running circles in my mind, crying like a nitwit. MATE!!! We found him!!!!!

My faculties were taken over by the most grounded fragrance of sage and I just gazed at him in shock, completely confused.

"Goodness my gosh..." Penelope murmured as she understood what had simply occurred.

Pursue snapped his eyes away and looked to his sister, "What?"

Gavin giggled, "Both of you?! This is great!"

Pursue shook his head, "Head higher up before mother throws a tantrum." He left with disappointment as I sat stuck to my seat.

Pause... for what reason would he say he is leaving? Aspen murmured

"I'm not sure..." I thought as I watched him leave the feasting lobby. I remained to follow him when the work chime rang and I let out a spat. "We'll see him later..."

I returned out to the field for the remainder of the day, buckling down on the collect. An hour prior to supper we were delivered for the night and I let out a long breathe out as I strolled down the long corridor to the end where my room was. I opened the entryway, my eyes tired and skin shrouded in a layer of soil.

I showered off the day preceding advancing toward supper, expecting to see Chase once more.

Chapter 2

Pursue

MATE MATE MATEEEEEE! My wolf cried in my mind.

I peered down at Maya with disturbance. I didn't need the little pack vagrant as my mate. I previously had somebody and had as of now intended to make her my mate.

I went through the day working with my dad, knowing sometime soon I would take over as Beta when the new Alpha was placed in.

"Pursue?"

I admired see my dad gazing at me inquisitively, "Well?"

"Care to express a feeling?" he asked, giving me an odd look.

I shook my head, "Yes sir.."

He watched with a smile as I attempted to sort out the thing we were discussing. "The clinical building..." he started.

"Indeed," I answered, "I figure we should place some consideration into it also. We've effectively had a few hardware wounds that would have been exceptional aided assuming the clinical structure was satisfactory."

The Alpha, Alpha-to-be, and my dad gestured their heads prior to turning around to their business.

You couldn't really be thinking about dismissing her?! She's our mate! my wolf hollered.

"We have a mate. Andrea is our mate," I answered.

He snarled at me prior to frowning toward the edges of my psyche. It was chosen. We would dismiss Maya.

At supper, I strolled in and quickly smelled her. Her fragrance was solid, occupying the room with the astounding smell of peaches. I was pulled from my daze when Andrea approached me, "Hello angel, need to go sit around there? I see a couple of open seats."

I grinned and folded my arm over her shoulders, "That's right."

I sat unobtrusively adjacent to Andrea, scanning the space for Maya. I at last thought that she is sitting with the twins. "Perfect..." I mumbled, knowing dismissing her wouldn't be simple with them generally around.

"Did you say something?" Andrea asked, setting a hand on mine.

"No," I answered prior to kissing her cheek. Andrea and I had been dating for right around a year now. She was the best, most considerate, most lovely young lady I knew. I realized it was stupid to succumb to somebody who wasn't my predetermined mate, yet she was everything to me. At the point when we hadn't observed our mates two years prior we started dating, trusting that assuming we didn't observe them we could pick one another.

Well that arrangement misfired, isn't that right? my wolf heaved.

I overlooked him and my eyes livened up when I saw Maya stroll off without anyone else. "I'll be right back," I said to Andrea, keeping my eyes on Maya as I strolled off toward the foyer she had strolled down.

"Maya," I called out as she arrived at the finish of the long foyer.

Maya went to me cheerfully, "Hey, Chase."

"We want to talk," I said briskly. She hitched her temple as she got on my terrible state of mind.

"Uhh.. OK. Enter," she answered, giving me an odd look.

I strolled into the room and shut the entryway behind me.

"Look Maya, this thing is-"

"I know it's not what you anticipated. I wasn't anticipating that it should be you," Maya said with an anxious laugh. "Be that as it may, I'm happy "

"No Maya, you misconstrue. I don't need this," I said, intruding on her.

"What?" she inquired. I could see she was confounded and frustrated as harmed crawled across her face.

I took a full breath, "I, Chase Branson, reject you, Maya Hart, as my mate."

NO!!! Pursue, don't do this!!! She is our mate!!! my wolf shouted as I said the dismissal.

Maya moaned as she multiplied over. I looked as she made a decent attempt to remain standing, tears tumbling down her cheeks from the aggravation. She took a full breath and gazed toward me with outrage. "I acknowledge your dismissal." She dismissed and strolled to the restroom, shutting the entryway behind her.

I recoiled at the developing aggravation in my mid-region, bowing down as I shut my eyes firmly, trusting the aggravation would end rapidly. Later a couple of seconds, the aggravation blurred and I fixed prior to strolling of the room feeling strangely weighty.

As I arrived at the finish of the lobby I grinned as I saw Andrea stroll toward me, "Hello! Need to head up?"

I pulled her nearby and squeezed my lips to hers, "How about we go."

She grinned, accepting my hand as we strolled higher up to my room.

The following morning was Sunday, our day away from work. The pack went through the day resting and getting to know one another. I strolled down the stairs for breakfast, seeing Maya wasn't there. I shook the thought out about my head, realizing she was most likely staying in bed. Not that I gave it a second thought, she was no longer my mate. Andrea was my mate.

I went through the day with Andrea, appreciating her conversation and keeping her in my arms however much as could reasonably be expected. I shut my eyes and took in her fragrance. She smelled decent, similar to coconut. Yet, I observed it wasn't quite so inebriating as Maya's fragrance had been.

At supper, we as a whole remained from our seats as the Alpha and Luna strolled in. "Aurora Pack, we are satisfied to have completed the gather season! Great work to all of you! Allow us to partake in the following seven day stretch of rest as we get ready for the following planting!"

The Luna ventured forward, "To an abundant collect!"

"To a copious reap!" the pack repeated.

I checked out the room brimming with pleased load individuals happily before my eyes laid on Maya. Her eyes were pitiful and I could perceive she was just grinning as a front. I took a full breath and fixed my hold on Andrea's shoulder, realizing I had settled on the best decision.

Chapter 3

MAYA

I remained outside the packhouse gazing toward the moon, holding my arms tight. I took a full breath and shut my eyes, envisioning a day to day existence where I had a mate who needed me.

"Maya?"

I pivoted to see Penelope remaining behind me with stress all over. I endeavored a grin and she let out a long breathe out as she understood what had occurred.

"He is a fool..." she said as she pulled me in for a warm embrace.

A couple of stray tears that hadn't fallen at this point slid down my cheeks as she held me.

She's right.. he's a simpleton... Aspen cried in solace.

Later a couple of seconds Penelope pulled back, putting her hands on my shoulders, "All things considered, I suppose you get to get the mateless club together with me and Gavin."

I laughed, "You're not mateless, you simply haven't tracked down them yet."

She shrugged, "Potato, potahto."

She tossed her arm around my shoulder and we strolled once again into the packhouse. Gavin went along with us and we sat on the sofa in the normal region for a film and truly necessary home base meeting.

As I laid in bed I thought about the most recent couple of days and how I felt. I was harmed and felt dismissed and undesirable. My wolf was disturbed, continually pacing in my mind, letting me know we ought to have battled for him. In any case, I wasn't going to battle for somebody who wouldn't allow me an opportunity, somebody who dismissed me without knowing me. Being dismissed had potentially been the most exceedingly awful aggravation I'd felt in my life. It tore through me like a blade, detaching the mate bond from inside me. I turned over in my bed at its prospect, pulling my knees to my chest as I shut my eyes and nodded off, indeed longing for a day when I would have a genuine home.

We had a whole seven day stretch of rest. It was my beloved season when the collect had been acquired and we got to unwind for seven days prior to clearing the fields for the following harvest.

I shut my eyes and accepting a full breath as I sat in a rocker on the entryway patio, partaking in the little snapshot of harmony.

"Maya..."

My eyes snapped open and I saw Chase remaining above me, the weak smell of sage actually waiting in my faculties.

"What do you need, Chase?" I asked with a slight frown.

Pursue grimaced, "I simply needed to perceive how you're doing."

I feigned exacerbation and turned away, "it doesn't matter to you how I feel. You simply need to realize I'm alright so you don't need to feel so terrible."

Pursue snarled, "That is not it, Maya."

I snapped my face toward him, "So what, then, at that point?" I remained from my seat with an episode, "You need to focus on it?"

"Focus on what?" he asked inquisitively.

"The way that you needn't bother with me. That we should be mates and on second thought of making an existence with me you chose to pick another person," I snapped.

Pursue ventured forward forcefully, "Whatever, Maya... clearly, it was an ill-conceived notion addressing you." He dismissed and strolled, leaving me remaining on the patio disappointed and alone.

I sat down and cleaned away the irate tear that tumbled down my cheek. I realized I shouldn't have addressed him like that. He was a Beta, he could have my stow away for being so resistant.

In the evening I found a seat at a table with my supper, trusting on the off chance that I held my head down I could simply go unrecognized and possibly move past this horrendous circumstance. I was shocked when Chase plunked down alongside me. I gazed toward him with a glare, "Would i be able to help you?"

Pursue shrugged, "I'm simply having supper."

I shook my head, "Find elsewhere to eat. You made it clear you don't need me, so disappear."

Pursue gazed at me briefly, "I was not kidding before. How are you?"

I breathed out, wishing he would let me be. "I'm fine, alright? You don't have to feel terrible, proceed to have your fun with Andrea. I've become acclimated to being undesirable."

Pursue shook his head, "Please accept my apologies."

I sneered, "No. You don't get to feel sorry. You dismissed me without even the smallest thought about the results. Disappear, Chase." I remained from the table and strolled to my room, still furious and hurt.

The following morning I woke early and got dressed, intellectually setting myself up for one more day of difficult work. As I strolled down the corridor toward the pack kitchen I was halted again by Chase.

"What do you need, Chase?" I asked, yanking my arm from his.

Pursue checked out me with limited eyes, "I don't have the foggiest idea. I just can't move away from you. For reasons unknown, I feel attracted to you and I would rather not be."

I feigned exacerbation, "That is the mate pull. It will disappear soon assuming that you simply overlook it. Like how I'm going to disregard you." I stood and left, wishing he would just allow me to live in my wretchedness.

Later breakfast I went to work, clearing the fields to set them up for the following planting with the remainder of the reapers. I gazed toward the sun, fixing my back as I let the sun warm my face.

"Maya!"

I went to the side to see Penelope running toward me, "Maya! You will have a hard time believing it!"

"What?" I laughed, entertained by her energy.

"We are hosting a gathering!" she hollered.

"Truly?" I answered in dismay. Aurora didn't by and large trust in significant gatherings and festivities. The main time we at any point had a major occasion like that was on the commemoration of the pack. We would have a major supper with moving and music. "How could they persuade the Alpha?"

"It was his thought!" she said, as yet endeavoring to slow down and rest.

"No way..." I answered, shaking my head.

"It's valid! Evidently, a couple of the adjoining packs are coming to restore their agreements with us so we are hosting a get-together while they are here!" Penelope screeched, clearly blissful with regards to the occasion.

I snickered, "Would you say you are invigorated on the grounds that it's a party or on the grounds that you get an opportunity to meet your mate?"

Penelope prodded me, "What is your take?"

"All things considered, when is it?" I inquired.

"Day later tomorrow! The house is in outright tumult right presently attempting to prepare."

I moaned, "There'll be no dozing this evening."

Gavin strolled over from where he had been working, clearing sweat off of his forehead as he moved toward us. "Both of you going to work today or would you say you are simply going to prattle about the party?"

We both stuck our tongues out at him prior to beginning back to work, discussing what we planned to wear.

As we strolled back dependent upon the house to change before supper Chase passed us, peering down at me as he folded his arm over Andrea. I had nothing against her, she was a great young lady. Yet, realizing he dismissed me to be with her annoyed me. What's more I don't think she even knew.

I passed them, attempting to be solid so he wouldn't understand how harmed I was. I strolled past, wanting to flee from here and never need to see him again.

"Maya?"

I admired see Gavin and Penelope gazing at me. "Gee?" I inquired.

"You OK?" Gavin asked as he watched his elder sibling stroll down the slope.

"That's right, I'm fine," I answered, "Basically over it now."

Penelope and Gavin gave each other a knowing look prior to murmuring back at me, telling me they didn't trust me.

"On the off chance that you need, I can punch him for you," Gavin presented with a grin.

I chuckled, "How did that work for you last time?"

Gavin's hand subliminally rose to his jaw as he recollected the last time he and his sibling got into a battle, "Not well."

Penelope snickered at her sibling prior to going to me, "Later supper come over and we can glance through my storeroom to track down something for the party

"Okay," I answered reluctantly, trusting I wouldn't see Chase.

Chapter 4

MAYA

As I sat on Penelope's bed watching her haul arbitrary dresses out of the storeroom, my psyche meandered back to the last week. I was woken up from my contemplations when Penelope spoke, "What might be said about this one?"

She held up a light blue dress prior to grimacing and tossing it on the bed. I chuckled prior to getting the dress, "I think this one is fine. It's your most pleasant one and the shading looks extraordinary on you."

She checked out it once more, "You sure?"

"Without a doubt," I answered, giving her the dress back. She let out a fit prior to searching for a dress for me. In Aurora, we didn't have much in the method of extravagant things. The pack drove a more straightforward, natural life. So our garments were all straightforward also. I looked as she took out another blue dress, this one undeniably more obscure than the first.

"This one.. it will look incredible on you!" she grinned as she gave me the dress.

I shrugged, "It'll work."

I wasn't by and large having a go at, realizing I had effectively observed my mate and that he didn't need me. There was no one at the party I would have to intrigue.

I examined front of the little mirror and breathed out, checking out myself all over.

"Well?" Penelope asked as she remained alongside me.

"It looks pleasant," I answered indifferently. I gazed at myself, my long light hair up in a curved mesh. The blue dress was short-sleeved and went down to simply over my knee, erupting out a piece at the base. It was straightforward yet looked pleasant.

"I realize you would rather not go this evening," she said, pressing my shoulders, "yet how about we simply go have a good time. Let free a bit."

I grinned, "you're correct, we should go live it up."

She scrunched her nose prior to wrapping her arm through mine, "I'm consistently correct." We left my room and down the stairs to the principle lobby. We strolled in and glanced around in amazement. The conference center was brilliant and noisy, loaded up with lights and individuals talking. We pushed through the group and advanced toward a little table where Gavin was at that point sitting.

"There you are!" he hollered, "I've been standing by for eternity!"

Penelope giggled, "We should get some food before it's completely gone!"

We wove through the group before at last arriving at the smorgasbord. "Excuse me," I heard from behind us. I pivoted to see Chase and Andrea joyfully remaining in line behind us. "Would you be able to snatch us a plate?" Andrea asked pleasantly.

"Uhh... no doubt here," I answered, giving her two paper plates.

"Much obliged to you," she grinned. I gave her a little grin prior to gazing toward Chase. He gazed at me, practically shocked. I didn't know whether it was on the grounds that I was spruced up or in light of the marginally off-kilter circumstance. I gave him a tight grin prior to turning around to Penelope who looked pale.

"That was awkward..." she murmured.

"Just for us! I don't think she even knows!" I murmured back.

Penelope panted, making everybody go to her. She hacked gracelessly briefly prior to turning around to the food. "I figure I should tell her."

"Don't even think about it!" I answered as we strolled back to the table. "Plus, he previously dismissed me. I'm almost certain there's no taking that back."

Penelope shrugged, "All things considered, it would teach him a lesson. I love my sibling however I could truly punch him at the present time."

Fall in line... my wolf, Aspen murmured.

As the evening wore on we moved and conversed with other pack individuals before at last sitting back at the table.

I hung over to Penelope, "I'll be right back, I want to utilize the young lady's room."

She gestured in answer and I took off the entryways of the lobby prior to transforming and colliding right with an enormous, transcending man.

"Gracious!" I heaved as we impacted, "Please accept my apologies, excuse me."

I turned upward just to be met with the most inebriating aroma I have at any point smelled. It resembled orange and cinnamon. My eyes were caught as I looked into the fresh, blue eyes of the man before me.

OUR MATE!!!! Aspen shouted in my mind.

"We don't have a mate... keep in mind?" I murmured. My face gobbled up when I heard a snarl.

"What did you say little wolf?" he asked, his voice profound and smooth.

I shook my head, not exactly knowing what to say.

"I...umm... I want to go..." I said rapidly prior to hurrying off down the foyer. I ran into the washroom, locking the entryway behind me. I inclined toward the entryway, my breath weighty, and my heart hustling. "What simply occurred?" I asked myself.

We got another opportunity!!! Aspen cried.

"Another opportunity?" I answered in dismay, my hands squeezed against my temple as I attempted to sort out the thing was going on. I started to hyperventilate. "I can't repeat the experience... I can't be dismissed once more... I can't-"

My frenzy was hindered by a thump on the entryway.

"One moment," I croaked.

I took a full breath and tapped my face prior to leaving the washroom, just to be met by the man once more.

"What do you mean dismissed once more?" he murmured, his face drawing near to mine.

I breathed in pointedly, my apprehension appearing on the other side, "I.. umm.. well you are my additional opportunity mate... my first mate dismissed me half a month prior when we saw as one another."

The man snarled and I pulled back, stressed that he was disturbed that I'd had a mate previously.

"Who was he?" he protested.

I delayed briefly, not knowing where this was going. "He... he's the Beta's most seasoned child, Chase. He didn't need me, so he dismissed me." I brought down my face, embarrassed that I was so undesirable.

Then, at that point, he left. I turned upward in shock as he strolled down the foyer and back to the party. I let out a murmur prior to strolling back in, realizing I was going to be dismissed briefly time.

My head gobbled up as I heard a shout. The group moved to uncover the man remaining over an oblivious Chase. I heaved, befuddled with regards to what was occurring.

The man approached me and folded his arm over my abdomen, pulling me near his side.

"Alpha Navaar, what is happening here?" Alpha James asked with a glare.

I gazed toward him with shock, "Alpha?!"

Obviously, he is! Didn't you feel his quality? It's so solid! Aspen spouted as I looked on in bewilderment.

He peered down at me with a smile prior to standing tall, "That young man annoyed my mate. So I showed him something new. You are fortunate I didn't kill him."

Alpha James gazed toward the man and back to me, "SHE is your mate?"

"Indeed. On the off chance that you wouldn't fret managing the pack move we will leave now. It was an exquisite party, Alpha James." He shook James' hand and took mine, hauling me out of the conference center.

I grabbed my hand away and gazed toward him, "I don't understand..."

"What could be understood? We are mates. You will go return your things and come once again to Eclipse with me," he answered as though it was only basic.

I shook my head, "However you don't-"

"I don't what?" he asked, venturing nearer to me.

I took a full breath, "You don't need me..." I brought down my face and my eyes shut as I prepared myself for the dismissal I knew would come. Later a couple of seconds of quiet, I woke me up to think that he is gazing at me with a frown. I gazed upward into his dark blue eyes with a touch of shock, "You're not going to dismiss me?"

He snarled, "For what reason would I do that?"

I shrugged, "It simply is by all accounts how my life is going."

He shook his head and it seemed as though he needed to say something, yet he didn't. I looked as he left, thinking about what was happening in his mind.

I made a beeline for my space to pack my things when I was trapped by a gigantic embrace. "Goodness my gosh! You can't be leaving!" Penelope cried as she held me tight.

"I can't really accept that you got another opportunity mate, and that he's an alpha!" Gavin said discreetly as he folded his arms over me.

I embraced them back, partaking in their glow. I pulled back, "I can't accept it by the same token. Presently come help me pack."

Chapter 5

MAYA

I left the house with my pack of garments. I claimed nothing else aside from a little image of me with my folks before they passed on. Navaar left from his huge SUV and strolled toward me, taking the pack from my hands. "This can't be the entirety of your things," he said peering down at my pack.

"I don't have a lot," I answered timidly.

"What befell the dress?" he asked, peering toward my holey pants and free tee shirt.

"It wasn't mine, I needed to give it back," I said, out of nowhere feeling extremely reluctant.

He snorted and set my pack in the storage compartment prior to opening the traveler entryway for me. I moved in and he advanced around the vehicle to the driver's side. As we drove down the rough country road away from the packhouse I let out a murmur.

"You'll observe things are distinctive at Eclipse," he said discreetly.

He was the alpha of Eclipse?! I started freezing intellectually, realizing the things said with regards to that pack. I took a full breath and gone to him with interest, "I've just heard tales about Eclipse."

Navaar smiled, "Whatever you heard is most likely obvious."

I shook my head, "So you truly do beat your little guys to make them heroes?"

He snarled, "No one has at any point been beaten in my pack." He stopped, grinning to himself, "Except if they requested it."

I let out a moan of alleviation. "Good..." I murmured. I had heard the reports about the Eclipse Pack. They were all champions, hard and cold and fierce. Their pack was generally metal and cowhide and fire though Aurora was generally light and development.

I was parted from my contemplations when he talked once more, keeping his eyes forward. "You're not an omega, I can feel that you're gamma-conceived, so for what reason do you have pretty much nothing? Who doesn't have any possessions?"

I jeered prior to glancing out the window, "Somebody with no family."

"No family?" he inquired.

"My folks kicked the bucket in a mishap when I was five. I've lived in the packhouse as far back as I can recollect, without help from anyone else except if I really wanted consideration. I'm the pack vagrant, so I was just given what I wanted."

He glowered, "That is silly. You ought to have been really focused on."

I shrugged, "It would have been great sometimes, however I lived." I glanced out the window, gazing at the trees and vehicles that cruised by.

We drove peacefully for an hour until at long last arriving at the Eclipse Pack's an area. I turned upward in wonderment, amazed at the thick timberland encompassing us as we drove down the cleared street, very different from the dusty country roads of Aurora.

"We're here," he said unobtrusively as we moved toward a gigantic stone chateau that I could accept that was the packhouse.

He got out of the SUV and snatched my sack, "Welcome to Eclipse."

I gazed up at the gigantic house. It was nothing similar to the basic farmhouse I had experienced childhood in. We strolled up the means, my eyes pretty much jumping off of my mind as I checked out the rich house. It was painted in warm tones with rich woods and stone. "This spot is delightful," I murmured.

I looked as a little smile crawled onto Navaar's face before rapidly vanishing. We strolled through to the normal region that flaunted a monstrous modern kitchen, an eating corridor loaded with long wood tables, and an amusement room that had every film and book under the sun. I followed him down a foyer fixed with entryways, "This is the pack residence. A portion of the single wolves like to reside here, just as fresh debuts that haven't been set at this point."

He strolled up the steps to the following floor, "This floor is our own. My office is here, just as the Beta's. You'll meet him tomorrow. He lives with his family on the following floor up."

I gestured quietly, as yet attempting to understand this monstrous spot. I finished him a bunch of swinging doors and let out a little wheeze. "This is in support of us?"

He laughed prior to strolling into the condo. It had tall roofs and rich tones. There was a kitchen and eating region just as an enormous front room with floor to roof windows coating the back divider, allowing in the twilight. We strolled beyond three different rooms until entering the expert suite. In the room was a monstrous bed with fresh white sheet material. It looked splendid among each of the warm woods of the room.

Navaar strolled past me and put my sack on the table in the little sitting region. "You can place your things in the storeroom." I grinned at him before unobtrusively advancing over to my sack. I opened it and eliminated my things, my photo placement dropping out onto the floor. I got it and grinned at it prior to setting on the table. As I set my garments aside and a couple of toiletries I had, I left, my eyes enlarging at the acknowledgment that we would be in a similar bed.

"I..umm..." I stammered, wavering by the bed.

He turned upward from the spot he was laying in with a grin. "Try not to stress little wolf, I won't have a go at anything."

I moved into the bed, sticking to the edge, "I truly do have a name you know… "

He had his arm resting behind his head and his eyes shut, "And what is it?" he asked unobtrusively.

"I am Maya," I answered with a touch of disposition, "And you are Alpha Navaar, right?"

He gestured his head, actually keeping his eyes shut.

"Alright... well... goodnight," I talked unobtrusively prior to moving to my side, my back confronting him as I pulled the covers up to my ears.

I woke toward the beginning of the day at five-thirty, by propensity, to wind up very near the man sharing my bed. My eyes enlarged as I understood our countenances were practically contacting. I paused my breathing, gradually stepping back prior to advancing toward the washroom. I turned on the shower, appreciating the delightful glass tiles as I moved in. It was the best shower of my existence with the high temp water descending from the cascade shower head and the steam quieting me. I moved out and made the way for the restroom gradually, hoping to ensure he was still snoozing. I crawled to the storeroom and immediately got dressed.

As I got out of the wardrobe I heard Navaar protest, "For what reason would you say you were up so early?"

"Please accept my apologies, I trusted I wouldn't wake you... it's a propensity I surmise," I answered quickly, unexpectedly feeling anxious.

He took a gander at me sideways, "What are you wearing?"

I peered down, "Uhh.. pants?"

He shook his head before his eyes spacey, mind connecting somebody in the pack.

I remained there confounded until a couple of moments some other time when there was a thump at the entryway. Navaar strolled to the entryway and took something from somebody prior to advancing over to me.

"Put these on," he said, giving me a couple of stockings and a games bra alongside some sneakers, "You can't actually prepare in pants."

I stopped briefly, "What do you mean, train?"

He feigned exacerbation at me, "As an individual from Eclipse you are needed to go to day by day preparing. It is considerably more required on the grounds that you are the future Luna. Get transformed, we should be down at the field in a thrity minutes."

Chapter 6

The last thing I had needed to do yesterday was go to the nonconformist compound. Their lifestyle to me appeared to be pointlessly basic. You can be a rancher and still be agreeable. You don't need to carry on with life wearing a burlap sack. Yet, observing that young lady had been an amazement. At 24 I wasn't hoping to find a mate any longer. I can't say I was excessively excited, having one of those hicks as my mate and my Luna. She would have an incredible reminder today at preparing.

However, i saw a sparkle in her. She had a fire in her, a strength. I laughed as I thought about her befuddled look toward the beginning of today prior to scowling as I pondered her circumstance. She wasn't really focused on by any means. She scarcely had any garments, and none were reasonable for life here in Eclipse. Particularly not really for a Luna.

In any case, she's so wonderful... we could generally go get her some garments... my wolf, Rango, murmured. He had been a goliath wreck the entire evening having her so close.

I feigned exacerbation at him. My enormous alpha wolf behaving like a little infatuated puppy. I inclined toward the entryway, trusting that Maya will change. At the point when she left the wardrobe I needed to make sure to relax briefly as I watched her stroll across the room. Evidently cultivating was a decent exercise, since she looked astonishing. The tights embraced her like a subsequent skin and her entire body was slender and tan.

Rango yelled in pleasure and I let out an awkward hack prior to leaving the entryway. "Prepared?"

She shrugged, "Not actually, yet I surmise I'll must be."

We strolled first floor and nearly made it outside until my more youthful sibling and Beta, Christian, hollered from the kitchen. "I didn't accept it when they said you tracked down a mate however here she is, flesh!" he blast with a giggle as he slapped my shoulder.

Maya gazed toward him with a brilliant grin, "Hello, I'm Maya."

"I'm Christian, I'm so happy to meet you," he said prior to lifting her in an embrace. I let out a compulsory snarl and he put her down with a smile, "So you tracked down yourself a cowgirl eh?"

Maya become flushed as I shook my head. "We should go, we'll be late for preparing," I said, pushing them out the entryway.

"So what was it like in Aurora?" Christian asked as we strolled down to the field.

She shrugged, "Peaceful, slow-paced, a great deal of difficult work."

He gestured, "Well you won't see as much peaceful or slow-paced here. However, we have a lot of difficult work."

I peered down at her and looked as her chocolate earthy colored eyes broadened as we entered the preparation field. The whole pack was there getting ready for this current morning's meeting.

I set my hand on the little of her back, sending shocks up my arm that I attempted to overlook, and drove her to the opposite side of the field.

"This is Maya," I disclosed to one of the coaches, "She doesn't have any preparation and should join the gathering of novices."

The man gestured prior to taking Maya and assisting her with tracking down a spot I strolled over to the gathering of lead champions and took off my shirt, prepared for a couple of good battles.

For the duration of the early daytime's instructional meeting I watched out for her, watching her bungle and hit with faltering. She was plainly not gifted at battling at all, yet I realized she would should have the option to shield herself or if nothing else deserve admiration from a gathering of heroes.

"Good day, Alpha," Ava, one of the top mentors, hollered cheerfully.

"Good day, Ava. Is everybody prepared for competing?" I inquired.

She become flushed, her eyes brimming with tease, "Yes Alpha, we are prepared for you."

Rango feigned exacerbation, When will she surrender?

I moaned, mumbling at the way that young lady wouldn't stop, "I can't really understand. Ideally she'll disappear later the declaration at breakfast."

Later a hard instructional meeting, we as a whole isolated for breakfast. I approached Maya who was gasping energetically, "How was it?"

Maya gave me a wide-looked at gaze, "Uhh... I think I have space for development."

I grinned, partaking in her demeanor. It was something contrary to what mine would in general be.

"Well you have the opportunity to improve at it," I answered as we approached the house.

As we went into our room she hurled herself onto the bed, "I'm never moving again. Just let me dieeee..."

I feigned exacerbation prior to strolling into the restroom and showering. At the point when I left she had moved to the sofa as she paused. She got up and went ahead in the restroom. She again left in her old pants and a tee-shirt.

"This will not do. Not so much for meeting the pack," I answered, shaking my head.

She peered down, somewhat deterred at my remark and I could see I had offended her a piece. I ran my hand through my hair, "That is not what I mean... I just... don't bother." I mind-connected Christian and requested that he send down his mate Shayna with something for Maya.

After five minutes, there was a tap at the entryway and Shayna strolled in. "Hello hun, is she..." Shayna followed off as she checked out Maya.

She strolled over with a comforting grin and gave her a warm embrace, "I'm so happy to meet you, Maya. You are totally wonderful!"

Maya grinned, pushing her hair behind her ear, "Thank you, it's great to meet you, as well."

She checked out Maya all over, "I presented to you a couple of things to wear until we can get you some new things. I really want to believe that they fit."

Maya strolled into the storage room and Shayna went to me with a wink, "She's pretty."

I grinned discreetly in answer. I needed to concede she was exceptionally beautiful. Her long light hair and dull chocolate eyes appeared to call to me, alongside that aroma of vanilla that blurred my brain each time she was close by. I raised my eyes when she left the storeroom in a structure fitted dark dress that embraced the ideal locations in general. I could feel Rango crying in my mind.

"Well?" she asked modestly.

"It'll work," I answered dryly, acquiring a glare from Shayna.

"You look awesome," Shayna answered happily.

Maya grinned brilliantly at her prior to taking the arm I offered, indeed sending shivers down my spine, and we strolled down to breakfast.

Chapter 7

MAYA

I was a bit nervous to meet the pack. I didn't know what I was walking into, having heard all of the rumors about Eclipse. We walked into the dining hall and I was surprised when it was full of kind, regular people.

"Eclipse Pack," Navaar spoke powerfully, "I want to introduce you to my mate and your soon-to-be Luna, Maya Hart. We will have the Luna ceremony in two days at the full moon."

The pack erupted into welcomes and smiles, excited to have a Luna. I smiled brightly, feeling welcome and wanted for the first time in my life. We sat down for breakfast, Navaar sitting beside me but not actually close enough to let our arms touch. We ate quietly. I didn't know what to say to him. He was just as hard as the rumors. I had seen him soften a few times but I couldn't tell if it was that or if he just had gas.

I ate slowly, just picking at my food. I felt a bit uncomfortable in my new setting. Navaar glanced up at me a few times but never said anything.

"Is it very different here from Aurora?" Shayna asked, making my head snap up at her voice.

I nodded, "Very. Back in Aurora, it's all simple and rustic. Here it's rich and modern. I've never seen anything like it."

"You never went to town?" Navaar asked.

I shook my head, "No. Only the higher-ranked members ever went to town."

Shayna looked at me curiously, "I thought you were a gamma?"

I nodded, "By birth. But since my parents died I haven't exactly lived that life."

Navaar growled and I looked over at him. For a moment I thought I saw anger but it was gone as fast as it appeared.

"Tomorrow Navaar can take you shopping," Shayna said with a sly grin.

I smiled at her teasing but I quickly stopped when I caught Navaar's glare. He stood from the table, "I have some work to do this morning. Come, Maya."

DID HE JUST TELL US TO COME LIKE SOME DOG?! Aspen hollered.

I looked up at him with a glare, "I'm not finished. I'll meet you when I'm done."

Navaar scowled, "Then you should have eaten faster. Let's go."

I let out a huff before getting up from the table and following upstairs to his office. As soon as the door closed behind me I was pushed up against it, Navaar's face just inches from mine. "Next time, do not fight me. Just do what I ask."

I glared up at him, not about to back down now, "Then ask nicely next time."

He narrowed his eyes at me, his bright blue eyes burrowing into mine. He turned around and sat at his desk. "Sit down and we can discuss your duties."

I folded my arms and cocked my head to the side. I was not about to move.

He let out a huff and rolled his eyes. "...please."

I gave him a tight smile before sitting down in the chair across from his desk.

"Since you were just a farmer, this is going to be a bit of a different experience for you," he began, looking down at his papers.

I glared at him, unamused at his choice of words. "Yes, but this farmer is the reason you have food on your table so I'd find a little more respect for the profession."

He gave me an irritated look before continuing, "Anyway...
I'll need your help with some of the administrative sides of
my work as Alpha. You will help plan events and meals as
well as continue your training."

I sat silently, expecting him to go on. He looked up at me
with a questioning look. I exhaled, "Yes, Alpha."

His eyes darkened for a moment and I scooted back in my
seat, unsure of what had just upset him.

"That will be all. You may go, I'll see you at evening
training."

I scoffed, "We train twice a day?"

He grinned smugly, "WE don't train twice a day, you do."

"Unbelievable..." I muttered as I got up from the chair and
walked out of the room. I turned back and gave him a sickly
sweet smile, "Have a nice day, Alpha."

As I closed the door behind me I heard him let out a low
growl. I smiled, now knowing what had irritated him, though
I wasn't quite sure why.

I decided to spend the rest of the day wandering around the
pack grounds. It was really beautiful here, the whole
territory surrounded by dense forest. I walked around,
exploring the rows of family housing and other buildings in
the area, most of them still nicer than the packhouse in
Aurora. In the late afternoon, I walked back up to the
packhouse, ready to rest my feet.

When I opened the door I was met by Navaar's dark eyes. "Where have you been?" he growled.

"I was just exploring the pack, why?" I replied innocently.

He glared down at me, "Why? Because I was looking everywhere for you, that's why!"

I looked up at him, anger and defiance in my eyes, "I'm sorry, I didn't realize I needed to inform you every time I decided to leave my bedroom."

Navaar glared at me, "Go get changed for training and be at the field in ten minutes."

I scowled at him before walking past, irritated that he couldn't just be nice. How is it that I had somehow won the horrible-mate lottery? One that rejected me and one who was a hard, distant jerk.

Maybe our mate was just worried about us, Aspen said hopefully.

I scoffed, "I doubt it."

I changed my clothes and walked down to the field to see Navaar standing in the grass with his arms crossed and a scowl on his face. "You're late."

"I am not late," I replied as I looked around, "Where is everyone else?"

He smirked, "I told you, everyone else only trains once a day, twice on Wednesdays. You will train twice a day, every day, until I decide you have advanced enough to go back to one-a-days."

I huffed, "Fine."

My eyes widened as I watched Navaar remove his shirt, his entire body hard and muscular.

You're drooling... Aspen teased.

I blinked a few times hoping to clear my mind, noting just how attractive he was. With his black hair and chiseled jaw, his blue eyes seemed to glow. He was tall and muscular from years of training daily.

"Okay, hit me," he said as he made a defensive stance.

I scrunched my face, suddenly nervous about having to do this with him. I took a deep breath and stepped forward like they had taught me earlier this morning, swinging my fist around toward him. He blocked it easily and kicked my feet out from under me.

"Again," he said from above me.

I let out a huff before picking myself up and stepping toward him again. Again, I landed on my rear. Navaar smiled in amusement, apparently he was enjoying this.

He stretched his neck, "Again."

I stood up and tried again, this time using my other hand to try and deliver a blow. He blocked it once again but this time when he kicked at me I moved out of the way.

"You're learning," he winked. I tried a few more times to get in a hit, only to be blocked. I moved toward him and was quickly knocked down, this time twisting around and landing in his arms. I looked up at him as his hands held tight to my waist, my hands gripping his arms. His face moved close to mine and I could feel myself being swept away by his scent. His nose brushed against my cheek, inhaling my scent. I could feel my heart pounding in my chest. He looked down into my eyes and smirked before dropping me. I landed on the ground with a huff.

He backed away with a devious look, "Again."

Chapter 8

MAYA

I woke up in the morning sore, my muscles screaming out to me in pain. I groaned as I stretched in bed before rolling over to see Navaar lying next to me. I looked at him with wide eyes, the mate pull daring me to reach out and touch him. I raised my hand, my fingers nearing his face before I jumped back at his low growl.

"What are you doing?" he grumbled.

"I...umm... you have fuzz on your face," I replied, lying through my teeth.

He opened his eyes and stared at me for a moment before climbing out of bed. "Better get up, or you'll be late for training."

I huffed, "When do we get a day off?"

"We don't," he replied as he walked to the closet to change.

"What do you mean, we don't? Everyone deserves a day off," I hollered.

"Yes, but the enemy doesn't take a day off. So neither will we," he replied as he walked out of the closet in shorts and a tee-shirt.

"That's ridiculous," I muttered before walking to the closet and changing into some shorts. I walked out of the closet to find he had left without me. "Rude..." I mumbled before making my way downstairs.

"Good morning, Alpha!" I heard that girl warrior call out as I entered the field. I rolled my eyes, slightly irritated that she would so openly flirt with him. But I ignored it and made my way to my group. All during training, I would look over once in a while to find Navaar watching me. I smiled, enjoying his gaze.

As training ended I walked over to him, "Ready for breakfast?" He turned and walked quietly up the hill. "Okay then..." I mumbled as I followed him up.

As we sat down to eat he turned to me, "After breakfast, I need you to come to my office. We need to go over details for the Luna ceremony tomorrow and the next meeting."

"Yes, Alpha," I replied, knowing how much he hated that. Not that I was exactly sure why.

As soon as we finished I walked with him to his office and took a seat in the chair across from his desk. "So what do you need me to do?" I asked, looking down at my notebook.

"Tomorrow is the Luna ceremony. You've seen one before, right?"

I nodded silently.

"Good," he continued, "This weekend's pack meeting is a big dinner, where everyone will get to spend the evening together to relax a bit. I need you to make sure the food and preparations are handled."

That's it? That's all the info we get for the ceremony? He's no help at all!! Aspen growled, clearly unamused at his quick dismissal of one of the biggest days of our life.

I nodded, "I can do that. How many people do I need to plan for?"

"We have four hundred in the pack," he replied, "Make sure we have everything we need."

"Will do," I answered, looking down at my notes, "Is there anything else? Like maybe what time I should show up to the ceremony?"

He shook his head, "Nine. Now, you can go."

I glared at him, "A thank you won't kill you, you know."

He narrowed his eyes at me, "Why would I thank you for doing your duties?"

I gave him a sarcastic look, "Because it's nice."

"Do I look nice to you?" he grumbled.

I smiled, "You can be nice to me, I won't tell anyone."

"That will be all, Maya," he replied as he looked back down at his work.

I scowled at him, "Yes, Alpha."

I heard him growl as I walked out of the office, the sound bringing a sly grin to my face. I spent the rest of the day working on the pack meeting. I spoke with the pack cooks and other members who would be helping out, finalizing details for the event. As I stepped out of the front door of the packhouse I closed my eyes, turning my face toward the sun and letting it warm me. I took a deep breath, letting the outside energize me. I had never spent so much time inside before, having spent every day in the fields back in Aurora.

"Maya," Navaar called out as he reached the door.

Good mood gone. I turned to him with a sweet grin, "Yes, Alpha?"

He growled, "It's time for your training."

I huffed before walking down the hill to the training grounds. Navaar removed his shirt and quickly lunged toward me. Without warning he shifted, his large wolf standing above me as I fell to the ground.

"What the hell, Navaar!" I hollered as I stood up.

He shifted back, "You should have been ready for that, you should have been able to protect yourself."

I growled at him, "I've only been doing this for three days. You can't expect me to just suddenly be an expert warrior."

Navaar stepped toward me, his solid frame towering over me, "Then pay attention."

I glared at him before stepping forward, "Or just stop being such a tool."

He growled, "What was that, little wolf?"

I narrowed my eyes at him, "You heard me. Stop being a jerk and maybe start actually treating me like your mate."

He threw a punch, narrowly missing as I dodged out of the way, "You haven't shown me you can handle it, little wolf."

I kicked at him, finally landing a blow to his side after days of missing every shot I took. I smirked, "Well, you haven't killed me yet. So how about you start being nice."

Navaar growled, "Why do you want me to be nice?"

I stopped with a sigh, dropping my hands to my sides as I met his eyes, "Because you're my mate. Because you're supposed to love and protect me, not just ignore me."

Navaar turned away, "Training session over." He walked up the hill and back to the packhouse.

I frowned and followed him up. He was going to hear me whether he liked it or not. "What is your problem?" I asked as we entered our room.

"Maya, just leave me alone," he replied.

I scowled, "If you don't want me, then why didn't you just reject me? Why bring me here?"

Navaar shook his head, "I don't believe in rejecting mates. A strong wolf realizes the importance of a mate. I'm just trying to figure out why we were given to each other."

I smirked, "Maybe I was sent to you to teach you how to quit being a stick-in-the-mud."

He growled at my words and turned toward me, his eyes slowly darkening. I let out a deflated sigh, "Maybe I'm here to help you be soft, to be kind. Because this whole hard, brooding warrior act is starting to get on my nerves."

Navaar stepped toward me, pressing my back against the door, "Who says it's an act? Maybe I really am just a cold, hard Alpha like in your stories."

I looked up into his eyes and touched my hand to his cheek, "I don't think that's true."

Navaar leaned into my hand for just a moment before pushing back from me and walking to the closet. I let out a long breath, hoping I would be able to figure out this mystery of an alpha.

Chapter 9

MAYA

The morning of the Luna ceremony was here. I was a wreck, nervously pacing my room after training this morning. I looked up at the sound of a knock on the door. Shayna walked in with a pitiful smile, "Hey... how's it going?"

I looked at her with wide eyes, "I don't know if I can do this. He's so cold, so hard. I'm not sure he even wants me."

Shayna sat on the bed with a smile, "Navaar is that way because he was raised to be that way. He is the alpha of the strongest warrior pack in the area. He protects us and everyone else. He had decades of slight abuse from his father being taught to be firm. Years of intense training and fighting have made him a bit hard. But just in the few days you've been here, I've seen him soften."

I shrugged, "I haven't seen it."

She smiled, "You will, just give it some time." She patted her thighs, "Now, let's figure out what we are going to do for the ceremony. Any way, in particular, you want to style your hair?"

I shook my head, "Nope. I don't even know what I'm going to wear."

Shayna grinned, "THAT I can help with." She rushed out of the room only to return five minutes later with a garment bag. "This is the dress every Luna in Eclipse has worn for the ceremony since the pack's founding."

She held the bag out and I opened it gingerly, hoping I wouldn't destroy it. My eyes widened as I pulled out the most gorgeous white dress. "This is beautiful," I said quietly as I held it up.

Shayna smiled, "It is. And it will look stunning on you."

As the day progressed I became less nervous and more excited about the evening's event. Shayna helped with my hair and makeup, curling and twisting my blonde hair into a braided crown and letting the rest of it flow in waves down my back. I slipped into the dress. It was a simple lace gown that was off the shoulder, with long lace sleeves and a fitted bodice that flowed to the floor. I looked in the mirror and barely recognized myself.

"You ready?" Shayna smiled as she squeezed my shoulders.

I took a deep breath, "As ready as I'll ever be."

We walked into the grand meeting hall and I was brought up to the stage. I walked toward Navaar, my knees suddenly feeling weak as I looked at him in his dark tailored suit. He looked handsome and fit and I could feel Aspen running in circles. I looked up at him to find him staring at me with a bit of surprise, clearly just as shocked at how I looked as I was.

He took my hand in his softly, leading me to the center of the stage. The touch was exhilarating and calming at the same time and I could feel my nervousness pass as he held onto my hand.

"Eclipse Pack, we have the pleasure tonight of making Maya Hart our new Luna," he turned to me with a small dagger and cut a line in my palm, doing the same to himself. He clasped our hands together and looked down at me, "Do you swear to keep and uphold pack law? To protect our borders and families, even with your life? To work hard to ensure our pack thrives?"

"I do," I answered boldly. A small, barely visible smile flashed across his face before he stepped behind me. I looked down at my palm to see my hand had already healed. Navaar pushed aside my hair, his fingers brushing against my skin sending a shiver down my spine. He looked forward, "With this mark, I make you official Luna of Eclipse." He bent his head to my shoulder and bit hard, breaking the skin. I winced at the pain but it was quickly replaced with warmth.

"Welcome to Eclipse, Luna Maya."

The pack burst into cheers and applause as Navaar offered his arm. I held onto his arm and we walked off the stage into the crowd of pack members. I smiled, feeling welcome and glad to officially have a mate.

At the end of the night, we walked into our room, undressing and changing into comfortable clothes. Navaar climbed into bed with a sigh and closed his eyes. I was surprised, usually marking also involved mating. I guess not, not that I wanted to yet. He hadn't exactly been warm to me since I had arrived.

"Well... goodnight," I whispered.

"Goodnight," he replied before rolling over and going to sleep.

Chapter 10

MAYA

I walked inside after an hour of being tortured by Navaar. I was sweaty, dirty, hungry, and exhausted. After almost three weeks of twice a day trainings, I was beat.

I walked upstairs and took a long, hot shower in an attempt to rinse off the day. I changed into a tank top and shorts and laid down on the bed. "I have an hour..." I whispered as I drifted off for a quick nap before dinner.

I woke to the sound of the bedroom door opening. I rolled over and closed my eyes again, not ready or willing to leave the comfort of my bed.

I felt the bed dip as Navaar sat on the edge of the bed. "You missed dinner..." Navaar whispered, pushing some hair away from my face. His fingers brushed my skin, sending tingles through me. I smiled at the touch, taking a deep breath before opening my eyes to see him sitting on the edge of the bed next to me. His hand rested on my arm and I placed my hand on it, savoring the warmth. Then suddenly the warmth was gone. I looked up at him to see him turn away and stand from the bed. I sat up and rubbed the sleep out of my eyes, only to realize he had left the room. I frowned before catching the most delicious smell. I looked down to see a tray of food sitting on the edge of the bed. I smiled at the gesture, hoping this was the beginning of him warming up to me. That he was finally showing real kindness.

I ate all of it, not realizing just how hungry I had been. I stood from the bed and walked out of the room and down the hall to Navaar's office. I knocked lightly on the door before opening it. He looked up at me with his bright eyes and I smiled, hoping he would return the warmth. He didn't.

"Thank you for the meal, I was starving," I smiled.

"You're welcome," he replied before looking back down at his papers. "I have a few more things to do, don't wait up."

I took a deep breath, realizing his kindness earlier had just been a lapse in judgment. "Okay then, goodnight." I left the room and went back to bed, falling asleep easily again, my exhaustion once again claiming me.

I woke up again naturally at five-thirty and groaned before rolling back over and closing my eyes. At six I woke again and I realized I was alone. I sat up in bed and looked around the room. "Where is he?" I asked myself, knowing he wasn't one to be up early.

I got dressed quickly, pulling on my leggings and sports bra with a loose tank over it before pulling my hair up in a knot on top of my head as I left the room. I walked out to find the apartment empty. I frowned and walked to his office, opening the door quietly.

"Good morning, Alpha..." a sultry voice spoke from atop the desk. I stepped in to find a beautiful, naked woman sitting on Navaar's desk. She looked at me with wide eyes, "You! Oh gosh!" She scrambled to cover herself as I glared darkly.

RIP HER HEAD OFF!!! HOW DARE SHE TRY TO TAKE OUR MATE!! KILL HER!!!!! Aspen yelled with fury.

I had to admit, for a moment I considered it. I turned and walked out of the office, anger and humiliation growing inside me. My mate was sleeping around, he had a girl on the side! No wonder he had barely shown me any warmth since I had arrived, he was already getting what he needed somewhere else.

I stomped outside, ready to smash some heads. I joined the group and began the warm-ups, determined to use my newfound fury in today's training. When we broke off into pairs for sparring I hit with fire and anger, my wolf threatening to break free.

I knew if I didn't calm down I would lose control. My eyes began to darken as my breathing became labored. My sparring partner smirked, welcoming the change in pace. She quickly shifted and her light brown wolf growled at me. I hesitated for a moment. In Aurora, you could never lose control like this but I found myself in this situation being almost encouraged to shift.

Let me out... Aspen growled.

I closed my eyes tight before exhaling and letting Aspen take control. We shifted smoothly, my black wolf giving a low growl as she and the other wolf circled each other. They lunged forward, connecting in the center with teeth bared and claws out. We fought for a few minutes, Aspen giving her all even though we had never fought or been trained to fight before now. After a few minutes, the brown wolf gained the upper hand and took us down. We shifted back, throwing on the spare clothes we kept beside the field. The girl shook my hand with a smile, "Thanks for the fight, it was just what I needed today."

I smiled, "Apparently it was just what I needed as well."

We walked over to one of the side benches and began wiping off the random cuts we had on our bodies.

"I'm Jayda, by the way," the girl said with a grin.

"Nice to meet you, I'm Maya," I replied.

"Oh, I know who you are, Luna. I was there at the ceremony. I was surprised to hear you're from Aurora. I didn't think they knew how to fight," she chuckled.

I laughed, "We don't. This is only my third week of training."

"You did pretty well for being so new. Come on, Luna, let's go grab some breakfast," she said as she stood from the bench.

I looked up at her with a smile before following her up the hill. We walked into the packhouse, talking about this morning's training before being stopped by Navaar. He looked down at me with a scowl, eyeing the cuts and bruises all over my body, "What happened to you?"

Suddenly my bad mood returned with a fury. I glared up at him, "I was at training, where you were supposed to be. What have YOU been doing all morning?" I snapped.

He growled down at me, "What is that supposed to mean?"

Jayda let out an uncomfortable cough, "I'll meet you in the dining hall..." she walked off quickly, not wanting to be witness to our angry exchange.

I narrowed my eyes at him, "It means that maybe if you hadn't spent the morning with your girlfriend you would have been at training. Now, if you don't mind, Jayda is waiting for me." I walked off angry, leaving Navaar growling in the hallway.

"I've never seen anyone talk to the Alpha like you just did..." Jayda said with wide eyes as I sat across from her.

I shrugged, "Well, he's being a jerk and I have a very low tolerance for that."

She chuckled, "I've never heard anyone call him that either."

I chuckled before deciding I was done talking about Navaar the grumpy alpha. "So what is it like here?" I asked, "I've only been here three weeks and I can already tell most of the rumors aren't true."

Jayda laughed, "Most of the rumors were made by the pack so others would just leave us alone."

I laughed, "That's horrible."

Jayda shrugged, "Well, Eclipse is a pretty powerful pack. We have a ridiculous amount of resources and we are paid well by surrounding packs to keep the peace. We train hard but it's just so we can protect ourselves and others."

I nodded, "So no monthly sacrifices?"

Jayda laughed, "Nope. We are a pretty normal pack. We just put a big focus on fighting. Because of that, a lot of the wolves here are a bit hardened but it's just a front they put up. If I'm being honest, we are actually taken care of a lot better than other packs. Our Alpha is hard and rough but he cares so much about us, making sure we always have what we need."

I knotted my brow as I thought about what she had told me. Maybe Navaar had been putting up a front too.

Sleeping with other she-wolves is not putting up a front, it's just being a dog... Aspen muttered, clearly still furious about this morning. I couldn't lie, I was still mad too. She had a point, there was a difference between being tough and just being a jerk.

"So is Aurora really as hippie-dippy as people say?" Jayda said with a laugh.

I chuckled, "And then some. At Aurora, it's all peaceful solutions and farming and living simply and rustic. Getting in touch with nature and the earth. What I did this morning... losing control... I would have been punished for that if we were in Aurora."

Jayda spat out her water a bit, "No way. You would be punished for getting upset?"

"They call it 'being unable to find a peaceable solution to my anger,'" I replied with sarcasm.

She rolled her eyes, "Girl... then welcome to Eclipse."

Chapter 11

MAYA

I made my way up to our room, to shower and change for the day. I stood in the shower, the hot water running over me and stinging the cuts on my skin. I winced as the pain triggered my tears. They began to fall down my cheeks filled with all of the anger and hurt I had felt all morning. It was just my luck that I would end up with two mates who both preferred other women to me. It hurt, and I was tired of being so unwanted. When I stopped crying I stayed in longer, hoping to rinse away my puffy face. I walked out of the bathroom and into the arms of Navaar. I backed away and looked up at him with a glare, "Excuse me."

He looked down at me with anger before softening as he took in my red eyes. "You've been crying... who hurt you, Maya?" he growled.

I scoffed, "You can't be serious..." I pushed past him and walked into the closet, closing the door behind me. I got dressed slowly, hoping Navaar would be gone when I emerged. I walked out and rolled my eyes with a huff as I saw him sitting on the chair in our little sitting area reading a book. I sat on the edge of the bed in silence as I slipped on my shoes.

"You going to tell me what's wrong?" he asked from behind a book.

I huffed before walking past him, "I have things to do. Go do whatever it is you do all day, Alpha."

He stood and walked toward me with a growl, "Maya, lose the attitude and just tell me what's wrong!"

I spun around, my anger boiling over, "You! You're what's wrong!! You think that just because I'm from Aurora I'll just let you walk all over me?! That I'll just let you do whatever or whoever you want because I'm a simple, peaceful little hippie girl from the farm! We're opened-minded there, but not THAT open-minded!"

Navaar stepped back shaking his head, "Wait... what are you talking about?" I could see him searching his mind for what could have possibly set me off and I huffed, irritated that he couldn't see he had been caught.

I growled, my eyes darkening as Aspen tried to push forward. I had never lost control so many times like this, I had never been so angry before. Navaar looked up at me and stepped forward and took my hand, his warmth radiating up my arm. The touch began to calm me and I could tell Aspen was soothed. I snatched my hand away once I had gained control, "Don't touch me. Don't ever touch me, not after you've touched her..."

"Her?" Navaar ran his hand through his hair in frustration, "Maya, what the hell are you talking about? Is this what you were going on about earlier?"

I glared at him, "Don't try and deny it. I saw her."

Navaar looked at me like I was crazy, "Who? Maya, I don't have a girlfriend."

"That warrior girl that is always around. I didn't realize it was because you two had some little thing going on," I snapped.

Navaar growled, "Stop, Maya. I told you, I don't have a girlfriend."

I scoffed at him, "Oh really? So then why was she in your office naked this morning?"

His scowl quickly disappeared, "Excuse me?"

I hesitated at his confusion before continuing, "You heard me. Why was she there if you weren't sleeping with her? You were gone all morning so I guess you enjoyed yourself plenty. Who needs a mate when they can have whoever they want, right?"

Navaar growled before walking out of the room. My breath caught as I watched him walk away and I sat on the edge of the bed. "He didn't even try to deny it..." I whispered.

We deserve better... we deserve to finally have love. We've gone too long without a real family... Aspen whined as I laid on the bed, unwilling to deal with the rest of the day. I knew I would have to see him later, that there was no avoiding him considering he was my trainer in the evenings. I closed my eyes and let out a long breath, "We'll just have to deal with that when we get there."

Chapter 12

NAVAAR

I walked out of the room in a fury before mind-linking Christian. "Christian, bring Ava to my office. Now."

Christian grumbled in response before severing the link. I burst into my office, pacing the room as I tried to rein in my anger.

This is ridiculous! You should have set her straight months ago! And now we are going to lose our mate because of it! Rango growled as I continued to walk around my office.

"She's so mad.." I muttered. "I've never given Ava any reason to think she had a shot. Why would she do something so stupid?"

We would be angry too if we had caught some wolf naked-in-waiting for our mate. You better make this right... Rango mumbled in reply. I knew he was right. If we had caught some guy waiting for Maya, naked and willing, we would have torn his head clean off.

My head snapped up when there was a tap at the door. "Come in," I growled.

Christian and Ava walked in. She smiled up at me, "What can I do for you Alpha?"

Christian turned to leave and I stopped him, "Christian, stay here. I need you to witness this."

Christian watched me with worry as Ava looked up in confusion. I stood tall and projected my alpha, "Ava, you have crossed the line and in doing so have upset my mate and your Luna. Let's get one thing clear, you will never let yourself be unclothed in my office or my presence ever again. Do you hear me?"

Ava looked up at me with shock, "But Alpha... I just wanted to..."

"NO!" I boomed, "You will never come in my presence again unless requested, do you understand?"

She lowered her head and spoke quietly, "Yes, Alpha."

"You may leave," I said with a scowl. She quickly turned and left the office. I turned to Christian who still had a dumbfounded look on his face.

"Wait... what happened?" he asked, finally making it out of his stupor.

I rolled my eyes before letting out a long breath, "Apparently, she thought she would let herself into my office this morning, naked. Maya caught her and now she's pissed at me."

Christian shook his head, "Man, I don't know what to tell you for that one. If Shayna had walked in on something like that she would have ripped her head off, and mine!"

I chuckled, "She just about ripped my head off." I looked at my watch and shook my head, "I need to go check on a few things."

Christian stopped me, "No, what you need to do is go fix things with your girl."

I let out a huff, "I need to give her some space. She's so angry right now she won't hear anything I have to say. I'll talk to her when we've both cooled down."

Christian followed me out of the office and down the hill. We watched as some of our top warriors trained and I decided to let off some steam by joining in. "You have room for one more?" I asked as I removed my shirt.

"There's always room for you, Alpha," one of the trainers replied.

After an hour of sparring, I threw my shirt back on and made my way down to some of the pack member houses that were currently under construction to check on how they were progressing. I watched for a while, trying to figure out how I was going to talk to Maya. She had been so upset.

You haven't exactly given her a reason to believe she is the only one... Rango mumbled. I knew he was right, but it wasn't as easy for me to just open myself up to someone I barely knew. I had been raised to be distant, to be hard. Maya was all soft and gentle.

I took a deep breath, deciding it was time to go talk to Maya, not knowing exactly what I was going to say. I walked up to the packhouse and made my way inside. As I entered our apartment I stopped for a moment, taking a deep breath as I mentally prepared myself for this. I had already been fighting the mate pull so hard. I hadn't been sure if she was going to last out here in Eclipse, but so far she had proved me wrong.

I walked in to find her sitting in a chair with a book, wiping at the random tear that would fall. I stepped forward, "Maya."

She looked up at me with a look of anger and disgust, "What do you want?"

I recoiled, letting my irritation get the better of me, "It's time for training. Let's go."

She huffed, "You really think I'm going anywhere with you?"

I stood tall, looking down at her with dark eyes, "You will come because it is the command of your alpha. Let's go."

She let out a small growl before walking out the door and down the stairs. I followed her, trying to keep my mind straight as I watched the sway of her hips as she walked to the field, reminding myself I was annoyed with her.

The moment she stepped onto the field she turned to me and shifted quickly, catching me by surprise as she lunged at me with her jaws snapping furiously. I stepped to the side, her teeth narrowly missing my neck. I glared down at her, "What the hell, Maya?"

She turned with a growl and walked toward the center of the field. Apparently, her wolf was angry at me as well. I smirked before shifting and sprinting to her, knocking her down as we collided. She yelped before locking her jaws on my leg, biting down hard. I winced at the pain, surprised she had bitten so hard. I got free and lunged at her, getting her neck in my jaws. She fought me, trying to wriggle herself free. When she realized I had her she whimpered in submission. I let go and stood above her for a moment before she shifted back. I watched as she walked to the bench and slipped on her spare clothes. I shifted back as well, limping to the bench on my bleeding foot. I looked down at it with a huff, she had gotten me good. She looked at me and for a moment I thought I saw worry as she glanced down at my foot. It quickly disappeared and she walked back up the hill without saying a word.

Chapter 13

MAYA

I walked into the room quietly and into the shower, rinsing off all of the blood and dirt from the cuts, scratches, and bites that had already healed. I got dressed and climbed into bed, not interested in going to dinner or seeing him for the rest of the day.

I closed my eyes, finally letting myself cry out my frustration. My shoulders heaved as I sobbed, letting out all of my anger and hurt. I had been so excited to find a mate, to finally have a real home and a family. I hadn't expected him to be a two-timing, hardened, jerk Alpha.

I stopped, sucking in my sobs as I heard the door open. I tried to keep myself quiet, hoping he would just leave me alone.

I stiffened when I felt the bed dip and Navaar move close to me. He laid beside me, careful not to touch but close enough to feel his warmth radiating. "Maya..." he whispered.

She sniffed before speaking harshly, "What do you want, Navaar?"

"Maya, I'm sorry."

"Sorry you messed around or sorry you got caught?" I snapped back.

"Turn around, Maya," he said softly. I shook my head silently, not wanting to look at him or have him see my face. "Maya, look at me," he said quietly.

I turned slowly, my face red and tear-stained. He pulled my face up to his and spoke softly, "I did not and will never have anyone else but you. You are my mate and I believe in mates."

I narrowed my eyes at him, "But that girl..."

Navaar shook his head, "Ava made a stupid choice and has been taken care of. She will not attempt to do anything like that again. I promise."

I looked up at him, searching his face for the truth, "Okay."

He looked at me with confusion, "Okay, what?"

"Okay, I believe you," I replied.

He took my hand in his, "Good, now let's go get some dinner before the pack eats all of it."

I groaned as he pulled me up out of the bed, "I can't move, I pushed myself too hard today..."

Navaar smirked, "Was that because you were angry at me?"

I nodded, "It was definitely because of you. I just about ripped her head off... and yours."

Navaar rolled his eyes before walking to the door.

That was surprisingly warm of him... Aspen grumbled, still angry at our mate.

"Yeah, it was," I replied, "Maybe he's realizing I don't need an Alpha, I need a mate."

I still hate him... Aspen growled in my head.

"I'm not sure I've forgiven him either," I whispered as I followed him downstairs.

I ate silently, still not feeling myself. I didn't know how tiring it was to be so angry. I felt drained, mentally and physically.

"So everyone is still alive?"

I looked up to see Jayda standing above me. I smiled lightly, "For now."

She chuckled before sitting across from me, "Are you feeling better?"

I nodded, "A little. I'm mostly just tired now. I think I'm going to head up early."

Jayda smiled, "See you at training tomorrow morning?"

"Of course," I replied, "Speaking of which, don't you guys ever take a day off?"

She shook her head, "Never. At least not since I've lived here, and I've lived here my whole life."

I scowled, "That needs to change. Everyone needs to rest once in a while."

She shrugged, "Our enemies don't rest."

I rolled my eyes as I stood from the table, "What enemies? Last time I checked no wars were going on. We should be able to take one day a week where we can spend time with our families and with our pack."

Jayda smirked, "Get to work then, Luna."

I smiled with a wave as I left the dining hall and made my way upstairs. I changed my clothes and crawled into bed, exhausted from the day.

I opened my eyes when Navaar climbed into bed a few hours later. I looked up at the clock beside the bed. Twelve-thirty. I groaned before rolling over and attempting to fall back to sleep. I looked up to see Navaar staring at me.

"Can I help you?" I mumbled before shifting in the bed to get comfortable.

He grumbled something incoherent before turning around so his back was facing me. "Okay..." I muttered, "Goodnight."

"Night..." I heard him mumble back to me.

The next morning I woke up and found myself alone again. I sighed before deciding that I was not going to get up. The dark cloud hanging over me from yesterday still hadn't left and I didn't want to do anything.

He's going to be mad if we don't go down... Aspen warned.

I shrugged as I pulled the covers up to my chin, "The only way I'm getting out of this bed is if the house is on fire. And even then, it's questionable." I rolled over and went back to sleep, relaxing in the warmth of my bed.

"MAYA!"

I shut my eyes tight, wishing I was anywhere but here. The bedroom door swung open and I heard footsteps stomp toward me, "Maya, you skipped training. And breakfast. Where the hell have you been?" Navaar growled. "You're still in bed? Seriously?"

I ignored him, pretending I was asleep. He let out a huff and sat on the edge of the bed. "Maya, you can't just sleep all day."

"Watch me..." I mumbled.

He growled and stood from the bed, throwing the covers back. I pulled my legs up to my chest as the wind from the blanket being snatched away surrounded me. "Navaaaaar! Stop!"

"I told you, Maya, we don't take days off," he said, walking across the room and sitting in the chair, taking my blankets with him.

I sat up with a glare, "Well, I'm taking one off! I'm exhausted and sore and angry and I just need a minute!"

Navaar rolled his eyes, "Go take a shower and meet me downstairs."

I crossed my arms, "No."

Navaar stood with a huff and walked to the bed, throwing me over his shoulder and carrying me to the bathroom as I yelled at him. He set me down in front of the shower, "Now are you going to get in and shower, or do I need to climb in with you and wash you myself?"

I gave him a sideways look, "You wouldn't..."

Navaar pulled off his shirt and turned on the water.

"Okay, okay, okay... I'll get in," I hollered, raising my hands in defense.

Uhhh why on earth did you stop him? Do you see those abs? Let him hold us and wash us and touch us!!!! Aspen howled.

"What happened to hating him?" I replied.

She huffed smugly as I climbed into the shower, attempting to wash off my weariness.

Chapter 14

MAYA

I walked downstairs to find Navaar standing in the entry of the packhouse waiting for me.

"So glad you finally decided to grace us with your presence, Luna," Navaar said sarcastically.

"I didn't have much of a choice, did I, Alpha?" I huffed before standing in front of him, "So? What was so important that you needed me to get out of bed?"

"Let's go," Navaar said as he pushed me out the front door. Outside the packhouse waiting for us was Navaar's dark SUV. "Alright, climb in," he said as he walked to the other side.

"So you've decided to take me back to Aurora, huh?" I said with a smirk.

"Don't tempt me," he replied as we drove down the road leading out of the pack territory.

I watched as we passed the thick forest, enjoying the scenery and quiet. We drove further past the territory and I watched as it all changed from forest to concrete. "Where are we going?" I asked as I looked out the window.

"I thought it was time to get you your own clothes," Navaar said quietly as he kept his face forward to the road ahead.

My face snapped toward him, "Really?"

"You sound surprised," he smirked.

"Well, yeah. I didn't think I would get more than the outfits Shayna gave to me," I replied.

"You can't think I would allow the Luna of this pack to walk around in the same five hand-me-down outfits every day," Navaar answered coldly.

I shrugged, "It's more than I had at Aurora..."

Navaar growled and I looked up at him to see anger flash through his face. It was the same look he gave every time I mentioned Aurora.

As we arrived at the outlet mall we parked the car and made our way around, walking in and out of shops with various bits of clothing.

I walked through the aisles of one store and looked at Navaar as he followed closely, grabbing random items he liked. "Why are you being so nice today?" I prodded.

Navaar looked at me, "I'm not."

I looked back at the racks of clothes, "Navaar, you've taken me on a shopping spree. You're being nice."

He smirked and turned back to the racks, pulling a few tops off the shelf. "Go try these on."

I took the clothes we had collected and made my way to a dressing room. I tried them on, enjoying the whistles from Aspen in my head before we bought them and went on our way.

"Why do you think Aurora and Eclipse are so different?" I asked as we walked down the sidewalk.

Navaar shrugged, "We just focus on different things. Eclipse focuses on the protection of our people, Aurora focuses on a more peaceful approach, which is fine. At Eclipse, we believe that you can be hardworking and still enjoy nice things. Aurora seems to think that to be down to earth you have to literally be covered in earth."

I chuckled at his comment and we continued going in and out of shops before finally heading home.

"Thank you for today," I said softly as we drove back to Eclipse.

"Mhmm," Navaar hummed as he focused on driving. I smiled as I watched him, his dark hair and hardened features seeming a bit softer today. We drove in silence, enjoying the calm of the ride.

When we got back to the packhouse Navaar helped me carry my things inside, setting my bags down on our bed before stepping toward the door. "Put your things away and meet me at the field in a half-hour."

I scowled, "I thought I was getting a day off."

Navaar smirked, "We don't take days off." He walked out the door and hollered back to me, "Thirty minutes!"

I rolled my eyes before putting my things away, looking at the full closet in awe. I had never had so many clothes before, let alone so many nice clothes. I changed and made my way downstairs and out to the field to find Navaar sitting on a bench waiting for me.

"You sure we can't just go for a walk and call it a workout?" I hollered as I approached him.

He turned around, his bare arms flexing as he looked over his shoulder, "Nice try. Let's get this done so we can go to dinner."

I let out a huff, "Alright."

He stood up, his shirtless upper body standing tall. I inhaled sharply as I took in the sight. I decided it wasn't fair for him to be the only one uncomfortable and pulled off my shirt, leaving only my strappy sports bra to cover me. His eyes widened for a moment before lunging toward me, swinging at my face with his large fists. I dodged him and threw a few blows, missing as well. We sparred for a while, each landing a few blows, before finally resting.

I sat on the ground, my chest heaving as I tried to catch my breath from the workout. Navaar walked to me, offering his hand to help me up. I took it, the contact sending shockwaves through me. Navaar let go quickly and began walking up the hill, "Let's go eat."

I let out a long breath, wishing he would just let me in, even a little bit.

We walked upstairs to change before heading to dinner. I showered quickly, just rinsing off the dust of the workout before getting dressed. Navaar walked out of the closet a little after I did and we walked toward the bedroom door to head downstairs.

I closed my eyes and took a deep breath, determined to press on with the crazy decision I had made as Aspen cheered me on in my head. As he opened the door I pushed against it, closing the door again before standing between the door and Navaar.

"Maya, what are you-"

I reached my hand up to his face and touched his cheek before pressing my lips to his gently. It sent tingles through my whole body as our lips touched. I could feel Navaar hesitate for a moment before he suddenly gave in and pressed me against the door, his hands gripping my waist as he kissed me deeper. He pulled me close and I could feel myself melting into him as his lips traveled down my neck. I placed my hands on his chest, the warmth of our bodies radiating through me. His lips crashed into mine again, kissing feverishly. I pushed off from his chest gently, my breathing static as I tried to catch my breath. I smiled up at him before opening the door and walking downstairs for dinner.

Oh gosh... Aspen huffed. *I'm going to be a mess for the rest of the night.*

"You and me both, babe," I replied breathlessly as I entered the dining hall.

Chapter 15

NAVAAR

I stood in the bedroom frozen to the spot. My brain was no longer working.

WHAT WAS THAT?! Rango hollered, high from the kiss that neither of us had been expecting.

"I have no idea.." I replied quietly, "But I definitely enjoyed it."

Where did that even come from? I thought she was mad at us... Rango howled, pacing in my mind.

"I thought so too," I said as I ran a hand through my hair. I didn't know just how much I had wanted that and now I craved it.

I walked downstairs to the dining hall, trying to hide the smile on my face when I saw Maya talking happily with Jayda. She had a brightness about her that was getting hard to fight.

I grabbed my food and walked over, sitting down beside her. I ate my food quietly for a moment before looking up to see Maya staring at me. "What?"

Maya shook her head, "Nothing..." she went back to eating and talking with her friend while I fought the sudden urge I had to place my hand on her thigh.

Just touch her.. it will make us feel better! Rango hollered.

I shook the thought from my head before finishing my dinner. I walked upstairs, knowing if I stayed near her any longer I would lose control. I sat on the bed, my head in my hands as I tried to get my mind straight. That one kiss had turned me into a mess.

Just as I started to calm myself down, Maya walked in. "Oh, hey," she smiled as she walked toward the closet.

"Hey," I replied, lying down on the bed.

Maya walked to the bed in a pair of extremely short shorts and laid down on her side with a book. I turned to her and looked at her for a moment. Her long blonde hair was falling around her shoulders, making me want to push my face into it and inhale her scent. I was glad we had bought her some new clothes. Every time I thought about how neglected she had been at Aurora I just about lost it. I let out an involuntary growl at the thought, catching her attention.

She looked up with a smirk, "Do you need something?"

My eyes widened as I realized I had been caught. "No, nothing."

I turned away, only to be brought back when I felt her take my hand. I looked down at the warmth radiating through me.

MATE HER!!! MATE HER NOW!! Rango hollered in my head. I shook him away, not knowing if either of us was ready for that yet.

"Maya..." I spoke quietly.

"Hmm?" She looked up at me with her bright eyes and I was lost. I leaned forward and pulled her close to me. I felt her stiffen, not sure what was happening.

I held her, feeling her body close to mine as the touch sent tingles through me. She softened after a moment, letting herself lean into me. I felt both of us begin to calm, the contact with our mates helping us relax. We fell asleep with Maya still wrapped in my arms.

I woke in the morning to find her still in my arms and I pulled myself closer to her, pushing my face into her hair like I had wanted to last night. She stirred, opening her eyes and stiffening once again. She looked up to my face, blushing as our eyes met.

"Good morning..." Maya whispered.

"Good morning," I replied softly. Before my mind knew what my body was doing I bent my face to hers and kissed her soft lips. She inhaled sharply at the touch of our lips before giving in and wrapping her arms around me, holding me close as we became more heated. My hands moved slowly beneath the hem of her shirt, moving gently up her rib cage. Suddenly Maya stopped, pushing away from me before I could go further. She smiled before climbing out of bed.

"Where are you going?" I asked, wanting her to come back.

"To get dressed, no days off remember?" Maya smirked as she turned and walked to the closet.

I growled, suddenly furious with myself for pushing daily training. I crawled out of bed and walked to the closet, opening the door just as she finished dressing, her leggings hugging her body like a second skin. I lunged toward her, picking her up behind the thighs so her legs wrapped around my waist as I pressed her against the wall. "I'm Alpha, I can skip training whenever I want," I growled as I kissed her deeply, her arms wrapping around my neck as she returned my kiss with her own heat.

Maya once again pushed away. It was starting to irritate me but I backed up, setting her down as she wanted.

"Why do you keep stopping me?" I asked quietly as I touched her cheek.

Maya smiled up at me, "You only started acting like this yesterday when I kissed you. How long would you have kept acting cold toward me if I hadn't done that?"

I shrugged, "I don't know."

Maya took my hand, "Exactly. You were cold and hard and distant to me since the moment we met. I need more than a few warm moments."

I exhaled, knowing she was right.

SHOW HER WE WANT HER!!!! Rango howled. I knew he wanted his mate, that this last month had been torture for him.

I held her hand in mine as we walked down to the training field, still craving that touch. Maya let go of my hand and walked over to her group of trainees. She turned back to face me with a small smile before turning back. That one smile felt like a punch to the gut, like all of the air was sucked out of me.

"Good morning, Alpha," Ava said quietly as she approached me.

"Good morning, Ava. Is everyone ready to begin?" I asked coldly.

"Yes, Alpha," she replied before bringing the group together for warm-ups. I watched Maya as training went on, enjoying how hard she was training. She was trying hard to work on her skills as a fighter and I was proud of her for working so hard. When training finished I walked over to her and bent my face to hers, "You want to go upstairs and change?"

Maya smirked at me, "You mean, you want another chance to make out with me."

I winked at her, "If you're lucky."

Maya let out a laugh before walking toward the house, "Come on, Alpha. We have things to do today."

I growled, still not liking it when she called me alpha. She went upstairs to the apartment and I finally caught up with her when we entered the living room. I pulled her close to me, my hands on her hips with her back against my chest, "You are the only one that gets to call me Navaar. No more teasing me with that 'Alpha' nonsense." I bent down and kissed her shoulder, making her hum with delight.

"Yes, Alpha," she whispered.

I let out a low growl before scooping her up and carrying her to the bedroom. I threw the door open and dropped her on the bed. Maya laughed brightly, "What are you doing?!"

"Take it back and maybe I'll let you get up," I said as I climbed up her body, placing kisses as I moved. Maya took a deep breath, clearly trying to keep her mind clear at the pleasure each kiss sent through her.

"Navaar..." she whispered, her voice breathy.

I smirked, "Sorry, I didn't hear you." I placed a kiss on her collarbone before looking into her eyes.

Maya smiled up at me, pushing away the hair that had fallen into my face. "Navaar."

I smiled down at her and kissed her lips. "Okay, I guess you can go shower now." Maya pushed me off and I rolled onto my back, "Need any help in there?"

Maya flipped over and sat above me so her hips were straddling mine, "I think I've got it handled." She placed a peck on my lips before hopping off toward the bathroom.

I sighed, wondering how she had gotten so far into my mind in just a few days.

Chaper 16

MAYA

It had been a week of shameless flirting and intense make-out sessions. I was enjoying getting to know my mate and finally receiving warmth from him. Every day we got closer to mating and every day I wanted it more. Aspen was constantly going wild in my mind, begging for us to just mate already.

I walked downstairs with a smile as I entered the dining hall. I grabbed a plate and sat beside Shayna and Christian. "Good morning," I grinned.

"Good morning, Luna," they replied.

"Where is Navaar?" Christian asked, "I'm surprised you two aren't connected at the hip."

I chuckled, "He had some work to do this morning. He'll be down in a bit."

Christian's face suddenly went blank and I watched as his face darkened. "Christian, what's wrong?" I asked.

"There's been some trouble at the border," he stood from the table, kissing Shayna on the cheek before jogging upstairs to Navaar's office. I sat for a moment before deciding to go up as well. I walked into Navaar's office just as Christian and Navaar began arguing about something.

"What is going on?" I asked as I pushed further into the room. Navaar looked up at me with surprise, "Maya, what are you doing here?"

"Christian said there was some trouble at the border, is everything alright?" I replied before sitting in a chair.

Navaar let out a huff, "The border patrol on the east side was attacked this morning. It's a pack we've dealt with before but they've never just blatantly attacked our borders like this."

"Who was it?" I asked, knotting my brow.

"It was the Red Moon Pack," he replied darkly. Clearly, there was some history there.

I shook my head, "Red Moon is nothing but skilled laborers, why would they attack a warrior pack? It doesn't make sense."

Navaar frowned, "It doesn't matter why, just that they did." He turned to Christian with a dark look, "I want you to prepare the first two battalions. We are going to send Red Moon a message."

Christian nodded, "Yes, Alpha." He left the room and I turned to Navaar with shock.

"You can't be serious. Navaar you're attacking a pack without reason!"

Navaar growled, "They came at our borders twice now, that's reason enough."

I frowned, "Navaar, listen to yourself. You are attacking a pack. That means women and children, families. You can't do that."

Navaar waved dismissively, "You don't know what you're talking about, Maya. You're from Aurora where everything is always sunshine and daisies."

I growled, "It doesn't take a warrior to know this is wrong."

Navaar let out a scoff, "So what would you have me do? Say 'please stop' and hope they listen?"

I rolled my eyes, "I mean if you think that will work..."

Navaar growled, "Maya, go do your own duties. I am Alpha and I need to make the decision that is best for my pack."

I glared at him, "So as Luna don't I have the right to weigh in on this?"

Navaar rolled his eyes at me, "Maya, you don't know the first thing about this."

I scowled, "That's crap and you know it. You can't just attack people."

Navaar stood tall, his alpha projecting through the room, "Maya, this is what's happening. You might be Luna but you don't know the first thing about protecting a pack. We are warriors, this is what we do. Get on board."

I glared at him, "If this is what you are going to do, if you are going to go attack innocent families because a few idiot wolves decided to make trouble, then don't expect me to stand by and watch."

Navaar' eyes narrowed, "Then don't watch." He walked around the desk and out of the office, leaving me angry and bewildered. I walked upstairs to our room to find Navaar changing out of his suit and into something more suitable for fighting. Not that it mattered since they would be shifting.

He walked past me, still angry. I took a deep breath and caught his arm, holding his hand tightly in mine. Navaar looked down at me with dark eyes, his wolf ready for a fight. I pulled myself close to him, resting my hands on his chest, "Navaar, please don't do this."

He pushed away from me and walked toward the door, "I have to go. I don't know how long this will take, don't wait up."

"I won't..." I whispered.

WAIT... WHAT ARE YOU DOING?! Aspen hollered in my head as she realized what I was thinking.

I heard the howls from the warriors as they ran gathered at the edge of the woods. I shook my head before I grabbed a bag from the closet and filled it with some clothes.

"We aren't staying here..." I whispered.

WE CAN'T JUST LEAVE OUR MATE! Aspen cried.

I wiped a stray tear off my cheek, "He is no mate of ours if he thinks it's okay to harm innocent women and children." I grabbed my bag and ran downstairs.

NAVAAR

When we shifted at the edge of the forest I could feel the power of the pack surging as we all prepared for battle. I took a deep breath, still angry over Maya's reaction. She didn't understand how things were done here. It was our job and our purpose to protect our people and the other packs we were asked to help.

She just didn't want to see others hurt. It's the reason you fell for her to begin with, isn't it? Rango echoed in my mind. I growled, not wanting to admit he was right. It had been her brightness and ability to be so kind and soft that had hooked me. I had never received so much gentleness in my life. I had been raised for one purpose: to be the hardened warrior Alpha of Eclipse.

"Focus..." I mumbled as we neared the border we shared with Red Moon Pack.

Rango growled in the anticipation of a fight. We pushed through the border, quickly taking out the few border patrolmen easily. We sprinted through the forest and I howled as the trees thinned, letting them know to be ready for a fight.

I stopped at the tree line and watched as my warriors lunged through the trees and into the open, colliding with male wolves I knew weren't fighters. I looked up with wide eyes when I heard the screams.

I could see the chaos and the fear as women ran with their pups into their homes and to the packhouse seeking safety. My eyes widened as I watched the terror in the faces of little children as they watched their fathers being cut down in an attempt to protect their families. Then everything seemed to go in slow motion as I saw a woman fall, her body lifeless on the ground as the warriors pushed forward.

"She was right..." I whispered in shock as I watched the scene before me.

Stop this before a child ends up hurt as well... Rango howled.

"STOP," I yelled through the mind link. "Everyone to the treeline."

My warriors obeyed, retreating behind me as the Alpha of Red Moon stepped out of the packhouse.

"Alpha Navaar!!" he boomed. "Care to explain why you have attacked my people?!"

I walked toward him, "Care to explain why our borders were attacked for the second time this morning?"

He growled, "Stupid kids..." The Alpha turned back to the packhouse as a group of young men walked onto the porch with their heads hung low. "Tell me you didn't do this!!" he yelled.

"We're sorry Alpha... we just-"

I stepped forward with a growl, "You just almost started a war because you wanted to try and prove yourselves against a few trained warriors!! You almost got your entire pack killed!"

The Alpha of Red Moon turned back to me, "I apologize for this, Alpha Navaar. This will NEVER happen again. I ask that you leave our land."

I nodded and turned, taking my warriors with me.

I ran through the woods hard and fast, knowing I had so much to fix, so much to apologize for.

"She was right..." I told myself again.

Yeah, she was! And now you've made her mad at us... AGAIN! Rango hollered, clearly irritated by how things were going.

I huffed before pushing myself harder, racing to the house with the hope I could fix this.

"Maya!" I hollered as I entered the apartment, my breath heavy from running. "Maya!" I called again, running into the bedroom. I looked around only to realize she wasn't there. I ran out of the apartment and down to the offices. When she wasn't there I checked the common area and even the training grounds. Nothing. I tried to mind-link her but I was blocked.

Apparently she's REALLY angry at us... Rango huffed.

I walked up to the apartment, deciding to shower and change while I waited for Maya to come back from wherever she had gone. After showering I walked into the closet and began to dress when I looked over to her side, realizing half of her clothes were gone.

I froze, unable to breathe as I realized what had happened.

SHE'S GONE!!!! YOU WERE A FOOL AND NOW SHE'S GONE!!! Rango yelled in my head.

I shook my head, "We're mates, she can't just leave... can she?"

Chapter 17

MAYA

I shifted and sprinted out of the territory. I ran hard for a long time through the thick forest of the Eclipse boundary before finally hitting the border. I pressed on, running through the fields of Aurora before nearing the family houses. I shifted back, my chest heaving, and my body spent from running so hard for so long. I slipped on some clothes and walked up to the packhouse. I knocked on the door and Luna Haven opened it, stepping back with surprise.

"Maya? I mean... Happy morning, Luna Maya. What brings you to Aurora?" She looked past me and around the front porch, "No Alpha Navaar?"

I shook my head, "I have left Eclipse and my mate. I would like to come back. I will work in the fields again, I don't care."

Luna Haven narrowed her eyes at me, "Why don't we go talk to the Alpha, hmm?"

I followed her inside, looking around the familiar packhouse, remembering the awe of Eclipse compared to Aurora. I followed her down the hall to Alpha James' office.

"Luna Maya, what can I do for you today?" he smiled, shaking my hand lightly. I knew the only reason they were acting this way was that they were afraid of Navaar. I sat in a chair across from his desk, "Well, Alpha, I would like to live here."

He shifted uncomfortably in his seat, "I'm not sure I can-"

I shook my head, "I won't cause any trouble. And I'm fine working in the fields again."

Alpha James hesitated for a moment, "Honestly, I don't think that will be possible. You are the Luna of another pack. Taking you in would cause problems for Aurora with one of the most powerful warrior packs in the country." I lowered my head at his words knowing he was right. He let out a long sigh before continuing, "But it doesn't mean you can't visit for a week or two. Welcome back to Aurora, Luna Maya."

I smiled, "It's just Maya, please. And thank you, I appreciate your help."

"You'll have to help in the fields, to earn your keep," Alpha spoke as we turned to leave. I gave a nod of understanding before turning to the door.

I walked out of his office and was led to my old room in the packhouse. I stepped inside, forgetting how different my life had been before Eclipse. I sat on the bed and cried, my tears falling hard as I realized my hopes for a family and a real home were gone.

In the evening my door opened with force, slamming into the wall.

"Maya?!" Penelope hollered as she ran in.

My tears began to fall again as I ran to my friend, colliding with her as we embraced each other tightly.

"I'm so sorry, sis," Penelope said as she pulled away. "What happened? Why are you here?"

I shook my head, "I don't belong there or with him. He made a decision today I can't get on board with, ever."

Penelope frowned, "That's ridiculous, he's your mate, Maya. You're Luna, you can't just leave."

"Well, I did and I'm not going back," I replied.

Penelope let out a huff, "You can't stay here forever and you know it.. Well, get a good night of sleep, we're up early here if you remember."

I nodded with a small smile before saying goodnight and watching Penelope leave. I sat back down on the bed and looked around the room, suddenly feeling very empty and alone.

I woke in the morning with a darkness hovering over me. It had only been half a day and I missed my mate. Being away from him was harder than I thought it would be, but I couldn't look past what Eclipse had just done. It was a long, hard day of work and I welcomed it. Working in the fields was a great distraction from my thoughts.

"So, are you going to reject him?" Gavin asked as we sat down for dinner.

"I don't think I can once I've been marked," I replied.

"You've been marked?" Penelope asked as she eyed my shoulder.

I pulled at the collar of my shirt, revealing the mark on my shoulder. "See, marked."

She took a deep breath, "Don't show that to anyone... I don't think they'd let you stay if they knew."

I nodded, knowing they couldn't just keep a Luna from another pack.

"So, no mates for you two yet?" I asked, hoping to change the subject.

Gavin shook his head, "No... I'm hoping it's just because they haven't turned twenty-one yet."

I shrugged, "It's true, they might not have a birthday until the end of the year."

"Actually..." Penelope fidgeted with her hands for a moment before looking up with a smile.

"No way! We've been together all day and you're just now telling me?! Who is he?!" I asked with excitement.

Penelope looked up and past me, a smile growing on her face. "Riley."

"Riley?" I looked at her curiously before turning around. Walking up behind me was the assistant veterinarian. He was a year older than us and had just returned from school, but he was cute and he was kind.

He kissed Penelope's cheek as he sat down, "Hi Luna Maya, nice to see you." He turned back to Penelope, "How was your day?"

They spoke quietly with eachother and I smiled as I watched them, glad she had found someone who seemed to care for her so much.

"Maybe some of us just don't have a mate.." Gavin muttered, pushing his food around his plate.

"Everyone has a mate," I replied with an eye

"Yeah, how is it that you've had two mates and I can't even find one?!" Gavin teased.

I lowered my face, "A whole lot of luck I've had with the both of them, huh?"

Penelope turned to me and took my hand, "Why don't you forgive him then. Go back to Eclipse and be Luna and have a real life."

I shook my head, "They attacked a harmless pack. Women and children. I can't condone that. I can't be okay with that."

Penelope shrugged, "Maybe there's more to the story..."

"I don't care. I'm not going back," I replied before getting up from the table and walking up to my room.

In the hallway, I saw Chase for the first time since leaving. Our eyes met and he looked at me with a pained stare. I looked away, no longer caring about what that man had to say. I kept walking until I was pushed to the side.

"Maya..." Chase whispered.

"Chase, what the hell are you doing?" I asked, pushing him away.

"You're back, that means you rejected that Alpha from Eclipse," he said quietly.

I shook my head, "No, I didn't reject him. Not that it's any of your business- I'm just here for a visit. What do you want Chase?"

He stepped closer to me, "Be my mate."

I laughed out loud, "I'm good, thanks though. Anyway, I thought you and Andrea were going to be mates."

He shook his head, "She found her mate a few weeks ago and decided to leave me instead of rejecting him, like I did for her."

I rolled my eyes, "That's too bad. Anyway, have a good night." I walked away toward my bedroom, not wanting to be near him ever again. Suddenly I was pulled backward, "Maya, take me back. I take back the rejection.. just-"

I growled, "I already told you. I have a mate. Now let go of me!"

Chase leaned forward and tried to crush his lips to mine. I growled before twisting his arm back and pushed him, using my months of training at Eclipse to gain the upper hand and get away from him. I rushed into my room, locking the door behind me with a huff. I leaned against the door, tears falling from my eyes as I thought about Navaar and how he had never tried to force it like Chase just had.

I missed him.

LET ME OUT, I'LL KILL HIM!! Aspen yelled in my head, furious that anyone but our mate tried to touch us.

"He was just confused... I don't think we'll have any more problems with him," I replied, wiping the tears from my face.

I MISS HIM TOO, BY THE WAY. CAN WE GO HOME YET? Aspen asked quietly.

"I don't think we'll ever go home..." I replied before falling into my bed with a sigh.

They won't let us stay. These are peaceful people, they won't dare upset Alpha Navaar... Aspen whispered.

"We'll just have to figure it out..." I mumbled.

Once again sleep didn't come for me. I found falling asleep hard now that Navaar wasn't in the bed with me. I didn't realize just how comforting having him near was to me.

I rolled over, wishing Navaar had just listened to me. That he hadn't been so hard or cold toward me.

MAYBE HE'LL FIGHT FOR US... Aspen whispered as I began to drift to sleep from exhaustion.

"If he was going to fight for us he would be here..." I whispered back, my heavy eyes finally giving in.

Chapter 18

NAVAAR

I paced my office, trying to focus my mind. She had been gone for three days. Three days without so much as a call or text or even a damn letter.

I ran my hands through my hair, my whole body on edge as I tried to grasp what had happened. My mate had left, disappeared without a word. "Where is she?" I muttered.

Rango growled in reply. Clearly, he was going to be of no help.

"She can't just run off... she's a Luna!" I mumbled to myself as I paced the room, my mind in chaos as I realized what I had done. She had told me she wouldn't stand by and watch me attack Red Moon. I practically told her to leave when I dismissively pushed aside her comments. I didn't hear her, instead of listening to my Luna I had pushed her away. I continued to pace, angry at myself, and angry that she had just left without saying anything.

"Idiot!" I yelled, slamming my fists into the wall.

YOU REALLY ARE... Rango said, finally speaking again.

I didn't sleep. I spent the rest of the night wondering where she was and how to get her back. Somehow in just a short amount of time, I had fallen for her hard.

I ran my hand through my hair, "I need to find her, I need to fix this. How did she leave without anybody noticing?"

SHE LEFT IN THE CHAOS OF THE ATTACK. PROBABLY SLIPPED OUT WITHOUT ANYONE EVEN SEEING HER... Rango replied in my mind.

The next morning I still hadn't heard anything. Maya hadn't attempted to even contact me, and nobody in the surrounding area had called to inform me she was there.

I paced my bedroom in frustration before throwing myself on the bed. "Where would she have even gone?"

Rango rolled his eyes at me,SHE PROBABLY WENT BACK TO AURORA.. THOSE TREE-HUGGING-

"That's exactly where she would have gone," I interrupted, "Why didn't I think of that?!" I jumped off my bed and walked out of the apartment. I jogged down the hall to my office to grab what I needed.

"Christian," I spoke over the mind link, "I have somewhere to be, you're in charge."

"Mhmm," Christian replied.

I grabbed my things and walked down the stairs to my SUV. I made the hour-long drive to Aurora, spending the entire time trying to come up with something to say to her. I had royally screwed up but at the same time I was angry that she had left.

I drove up the dirt road that led to Aurora's packhouse. As I pulled up I saw Alpha James step out onto the porch. I climbed out of the car, putting on my diplomatic hat. "Hello Alpha. I've come for my mate, can you bring her to me?"

He shook his head, "I apologize Alpha Navaar, but she's requested to be left alone."

I growled, "She's my mate. You have no right to keep her from me."

James shrugged, "I'm sorry, Alpha. I really am. But she made it clear she wants to leave Eclipse and the harshness there. Now, I told her we couldn't keep her from her mate, but I have allowed her a two-week long stay. Please be respectful."

My jaw clenched as I tried to keep Rango at bay, "Just let me speak to her."

"I'm sorry you drove all this way, Alpha Navaar. I'll make sure to tell her you came."

I glared at him before looking around us at the fields, wondering if there was a way I could sneak into the packhouse. As I looked out across the farm I saw her. She was standing in the middle of a field of green beans in her holey jeans and a ragged tee-shirt.

"Maya... please..." I called out through the mind-link as I walked toward the field. I could tell she was blocking me, that she didn't want to speak to me. I tried again though, hoping to crack through her shell. "Maya, please just let me talk to you."

"I have nothing to say Navaar, leave..." she whispered back before walking away further into the field and closing her mind to me. I growled and got back in the car, hoping if I gave her some space to think she would be more willing to talk to me. I drove back down the dirt road, feeling empty as I returned home without my mate.

MAYA

I watched as he drove away and wiped a tear from my cheek. I went back to work, part of me still furious with him and part of me wanting to go back with him.

I turned back to my work to see Gavin and Penelope staring at me with pitiful looks.

"What?" I snapped.

They both shook their heads, neither one wanting to comment.

I had been back at Aurora for a little over a week. I would be lying if I said I didn't miss Eclipse. I hated farming, but it was better than living with a pack who thought unnecessary violence was okay. And yet I found myself missing him. I stood and turned my face toward the sun, the heat beating down on me. I closed my eyes and enjoyed the warmth for a moment until that moment was interrupted.

"Maya..."

I turned around to see Chase standing behind me. I rolled my eyes in frustration, "Chase, what do you want?"

He looked down, kicking some pebbles on the ground, "Maya, I need a second chance, I need you to forgive me."

I narrowed my eyes at him, "Like the chance you didn't give me?" I turned away from Chase, my anger evident in my eyes, "You didn't know me and yet immediately decided you didn't want me. The only reason you're here groveling is because Andrea made the smart choice and went with her destined mate."

Chase shook his head, "No... I-"

I waved my hand at him dismissively, "No. You don't get to decide you want me now. I've moved on now just leave me alone."

Chase took my hand in his, "Let me try again, let me get it right this time."

I looked at him, noting the sadness in his eyes before they were replaced with something else that almost looked like fear.

My thoughts were swiftly interrupted when Chase was pummeled to the ground. I stood in shock for a moment until my brain caught up and took in the scene before me. I shook my head and looked up at Navaar with a scowl.

"What the hell, Navaar?!" I yelled.

He looked down at Chase with a dark growl, "You so much as BREATHE near my mate again, little Beta, and I'll rip you to pieces." His fury was then focused on me, his dark eyes glaring into mine, "And what the hell do you think you were doing, letting him touch you like that?"

I glared at him with anger. "I was taking care of it, Alpha! Why are you here?" I asked as I helped Chase off the ground and watched him walk back up to the packhouse. I turned to face Navaar, the fury in my eyes matching his own.

Navaar straightened himself, "I came to take you home."

I shook my head, "I'm not going home with you."

"Like hell, you aren't!" he hollered. "You're my mate, Maya. Now grab your stuff, let's go." He took my hand and began walking down the row of crops.

I yanked my hand away, "You haven't changed! Do you even understand why I left?!"

Navaar's face darkened, "I know why. And I was willing to talk with you about it but now that I see you're just trying to mess around with that poor excuse for a Beta my patience is gone. Get in the car."

I crossed my arms and stood my ground, "No."

"Get in the damn car, Maya!" he yelled.

"I'm not going back! Not after you cold-heartedly wiped out a pack! I will not be a part of that! Goodbye, Navaar!" I yelled before walking into the packhouse.

I watched out the window as he shifted and ran into the trees, once again wiping the tears from my face. Being so close to him, feeling his touch, and breathing in his scent had sent a fire through me. I missed him now more than ever.

Let's forgive him and go home... Aspen whined.

"No," I replied, "I miss him but he crossed a line I'm not willing to accept."

Chapter 19

NAVAAR

17 days.

She had been gone for two and a half weeks. I had tried so many times to get her to come home. I sat at my desk in my office with my head in my hands, wishing I knew how to make this right.

She was so angry, so hurt. I hadn't listened to her. I had gone into autopilot. Years of training had taught me what to do in that situation and I didn't think that there might have been a different solution.

I missed her. I could feel myself going crazy without her. I didn't realize just how much I had come to need her, almost like a drug.

I paced my office for a moment before realizing what I needed to do. I grabbed my things and headed down to my car.

"Let's hope this works..." I mumbled to myself as I drove out of the territory toward Aurora.

It better... Rango growled.

MAYA

I stood in the middle of the field and looked up at the sun beating down on me. I closed my eyes and took a deep breath before my mind was interrupted. I could feel someone trying to get in my mind. I turned around to see Navaar standing behind me. My eyes widened as I looked up at him.

"Maya, please just let me talk to you," he said softly.

"Navaar, go away," I huffed and turned away, walking down to the row and hoping he would drop it and let me be. I was suddenly pulled backward, swinging around to see Navaar standing above me. I looked up at him with fury. "I said, go away."

Navaar's face softened, "Maya, I made a mistake. I shouldn't have attacked them, I should have listened to what you were saying..."

I pulled away from him, "I know that! I told you I wouldn't stand by and watch you do that. I asked you to stop, to not go through with it. But you were too bull-headed and proud! You might be a warrior but it doesn't mean you have to be so hard all the time!" I yelled at him loudly, the whole field witnessing our little fight.

Navaar growled, "Would you just come home so we can talk about this?"

"I'm not going anywhere with you, Alpha!" I hollered.

His eyes darkened at my words and I knew calling him alpha had had its desired effect. He turned and walked away and I glared at his retreating form before turning back to my work. I worked for the rest of the day before hearing the dinner bell ring. I let out a long sigh before making my way up to the house, dirty and exhausted. As I stepped onto the porch I looked up to see Navaar sitting in a rocking chair off to the side. I tried to ignore him but when my eyes met his dark blue ones I gave in.

"I thought I told you to leave," I said as I stood above him.

He took my hand and lowered his head as he spoke calmly, "I didn't attack them..."

My brow furrowed as I heard him, "What did you say?"

Navaar stood from the chair and stepped toward me, our bodies almost touching. "I said I didn't attack them. I mean, I did, but I stopped it. When we reached Red Moon I let the warriors loose. I watched as they attacked families, I watched as women and pups ran away with terror and I knew you were right. So I stopped it. I pulled them back and talked peacefully with the Alpha and then we left. I ran home as fast as I could to fix it, to tell you..." Navaar lowered his head again, "...to tell you I'm sorry."

Oh gosh... forgive him! Forgive him and let's have that man's pups! Aspen whistled in my head. I rolled my eyes at her before looking up at Navaar.

"You pushed me away. You can't just be so dismissive and then expect me to come running back to you. How do I know you won't just do it again the next time you feel some threat?" I asked.

Navaar shrugged, "You don't. But I promise that next time I'll listen and take what you have to say in mind when I make that choice."

I looked up at him before shaking my head, "No. I'm finished with warriors. I can't live a life full of hardness and anger."

I let out a gasp as Navaar pulled me close so my hands were pressed up against his hard chest. He bent his head to my ear and spoke low, "Help me learn to be soft..."

I shivered, knowing he had just won. I pushed off and walked down the long wrap-around porch, "I can't just go back and have everything return to the way it was."

Navaar followed, "Maya, I'm sorry... I know I messed up. What do you want me to do?"

I narrowed my eyes, "I want Sundays off."

"Fine."

"For everyone," I said with a smirk.

Navaar growled, "Fine."

"And I want to be in every meeting," I said, hoping if I sounded confident he wouldn't know I was a hot mess inside.

Navaar clenched his jaw, "Fine."

"And I want-"

Navaar's lips crushed to mine, interrupting my list of demands. I hesitated a moment before giving in and wrapping my arms around his neck. "Let's go home," he whispered.

"Let me go grab my things," I replied, letting go of him and walking toward the door.

"Don't," he replied, pulling me back to him, "We'll just get you new things when we get home."

I shook my head with a chuckle, "You're crazy, it'll only take a minute."

"That's a minute longer than I want to be here," he replied, walking down the front steps.

Navaar took my hand and we walked to the SUV together. When he climbed in the car he took my hand in his as we made the drive home.

As we pulled up I took a deep breath before stepping out of the SUV. Navaar walked around and took my hand before taking me inside.

"Luna!" Christian hollered as we walked through the door.

"Hey Christian," I replied with a smile.

"I'm glad you're back," he said with a smirk, "this guy has been a grump for weeks."

Navaar rolled his eyes before taking me upstairs. As we entered the apartment Navaar pulled me close, wrapping his arms around my waist tightly. "You can't leave like that ever again," he whispered before kissing me deeply.

I wove my arms around his neck before pulling back with a smirk, "Then don't do any more stupid things, Alpha."

He growled, "I'm sorry... I think I misheard you. I thought I heard you call me Alpha."

I smiled before kissing his lips, "I most definitely called you Alpha."

He pulled me up, my legs wrapping around his waist as he pressed me gently against the wall. He kissed my neck, making me moan lightly in response as his hands slowly moved up my thighs, playing with the hem of my shorts.

"Maybe we should talk about-"

"Later..." Navaar interrupted. "I missed my mate."

I pushed on his chest as I tried to clear my mind.

Aspen was going wild, *WOULD YOU QUIT STOPPING?! Jump his bones already!!!!!* She yelled at me.

I shook her out of my mind before looking into Navaar's deep blue eyes. "First, we need to talk about what happened."

Navaar groaned before setting me down. I took his hand and walked to the couch. "Navaar, I need a home. Not just a mate who occasionally shows me some attention and kindness. Are you ready for that?"

Navaar looked down, "I am, Maya. I didn't know just how much I needed it until you were gone. It might be a bit of a rough change for me. I was never shown anything but how to be hard... I need you to try and be patient with me. I was never taught how to be gentle."

"I'll try," I replied with a wink.

"But I have a few requests of my own..." Navaar said quietly.

"Oh really?" I replied with a bit of sass.

"Well for starters, I need you to promise not to run off to Aurora every time you're mad at me."

I rolled my eyes, "Well as long as you don't try destroying an entire pack again."

Navaar exhaled and I could tell he was a bit frustrated. "That brings me to my second point. Maya, this is a warrior pack. At some point, we will have to help with pack wars or disputes or whatever nonsense other packs get themselves into. And I need you to understand that we are just doing our job. The packs have made their choice when they decide to go to war, and Eclipse is called in to handle things. People are going to get hurt, it's just the way it is."

I lowered my head, knowing he was right. "I understand... I don't like it, but I understand."

"Thank you," he replied. He slapped his legs, "Now, let's head down to lunch. I know a certain pack that has missed its Luna."

I smiled up at him before being pulled off the couch. We headed downstairs to find the whole pack ready to greet us.

"Welcome home, Luna!" Jayda hollered as she hugged me tightly.

"Thanks, Jayda," I chuckled, looking up at Navaar with a smile.

Chapter 20

NAVAAR

I watched as Maya talked happily with Christian and Shayna. They were all laughing and making jokes and I enjoyed the brightness she brought to the pack and my home. I looked down at my watch and let out a long breath before placing a hand on her back. "Are you ready to head up?" I asked, ready to have some time alone with my mate.

She looked at me with a smile, "Yep." Maya then turned back to my brother and his wife and told them goodnight before taking my hand and following me upstairs.

As we walked into our room I closed the door before pulling Maya close to me. "Maya, I don't think you understand just how much I missed you. Two weeks without seeing your face or touching your skin..." I whispered as I brushed my fingers up and down her arms. I felt her shiver before looking up into my eyes.

"I missed you too, Navaar," she said quietly.

I lost it. My lips crushed to hers, wanting so badly to make up for the last six weeks of not being together. Maya kissed me back with a fever as we removed each other's clothes. I picked her up , her legs wrapping around my waist as I walked the bed, setting her down gently before climbing above her. Maya let out a quiet moan as my hands wandered her body before letting them rest on her hips. Her warm lips sending sparks through my body. Maya moaned as I kissed and licked at her mark, my lips making their way down her body. I let my tongue tease her outer walls, making her moan again before sucking her bud, enjoying the taste of her, and moving my fingers slowly inside her. She arched her back in pleasure as I took my fingers in and out, the pressure building up. "Navaar.." she moaned as she released, the sound of her saying my name driving me crazy. I moved back up her body, attempting to kiss every inch of her. I crushed my lips to hers, our tongues taking in the taste of each other. I teased her again, this time with my tip, and a low growl escaped my lips as she ground her hips against mine.

I pushed into her slowly, her body tight and wet. Maya moaned, digging her fingers into my back. She kissed me with passion, her hands brushing across my chest as I moved above her, thrusting myself in and out as we both felt the pleasure building. I could feel myself on the edge and I bit down on my mark, sending pleasure through Maya's body. She pulled me close and as I was about to give in she marked me, the small pinch of pain overwhelmed by warmth and pleasure, making me release.

We laid together, Maya's head resting on my chest as I held her in my arms, glad my mate was back home with me.

"Navaar?"

"Hmm?" I replied softly.

"I'm sorry I just left without saying anything. I should have waited to hear the whole story," she spoke quietly.

"Thank you," I said before placing a gentle kiss on her lips.

In the morning I woke up to see Maya wasn't in bed. I panicked and for a moment thought it had all been a dream. I jumped out of bed and searched the room, my mind going to a thousand different dark places as I tried to find her.

I walked out of the bedroom and let out a sigh of relief when I found her standing in the kitchen of our apartment. I walked up to Maya and stood behind her, wrapping my arms around her waist and resting my head on her shoulder. "I thought you left again..." I whispered, kissing her mark.

Maya leaned into me with a happy sigh, "I woke up early and didn't want to wake you. Coffee?"

"Yes, please," I replied as I took the cup from her. I leaned against the counter and smiled at my mate, glad she was back and that I had let her in. "What do you say about going to dinner tonight?" I asked.

Maya turned to me with surprise, "Really?"

"Why do you sound so surprised?" I teased.

Maya chuckled, "You do remember yourself from when we first met, right? The brooding, cold, hardened warrior Alpha who didn't have time for his mate."

I huffed before pulling her close to me, "I told you, I'm trying to be the mate you deserve."

Maya smirked up at me, "And what do I deserve?"

I growled as I kissed her softly before lifting her onto the kitchen counter, moving my hands up her bare thighs and playing with the hem of her shorts. Maya kissed my lips, knotting her hands into my hair, her body responding to my touch.

"Alpha..."

I groaned, "What?" I hollered through the mind link.

Maya gave me a weird look before realizing I wasn't talking to her.

"We got a call from a pack to the south that needs assistance with a border dispute."

I rolled my eyes. "Send two battalions over to help them," I replied before severing the link and turning back to Maya. "Where were we?" I whispered.

Maya giggled into my kiss, "We were on our way to training."

I lowered my face in defeat, "You're trying to drive me crazy."

Maya smirked before hopping off the counter, her body rubbing against mine as she moved, sending shockwaves through me.

"Don't worry, Alpha. Tomorrow we get the whole day off," she winked as she walked out of the apartment.

I ran my hand through my hair, not knowing how I had fallen so hard for that woman.

Chapter 21

MAYA

I grinned as I plunked down opposite Jayda subsequent to preparing.

"You are apparently progressing admirably, Luna," she smiled.

"I'm, really," I answered with backtalk.

"Happy you're back," Jayda grinned.

"I'm as well," I answered. "How have things been while I was no more?"

Jayda shrugged, "Normal, worn out, normal, worn out. Preparing and such."

I looked into when Navaar strolled in and remained alongside him for his declaration. "Overshadow Pack, I have a couple of declarations. Above all else, welcome home to Luna Maya. We as a whole missed you." Navaar kissed my hand prior to proceeding, "Additionally, from this point forward, the whole pack will have Sundays off. No preparation or gatherings. Partake in some vacation and have a great time."

The pack applauded, energized for the new change. I gazed toward Navaar with a smile, happy to be home.

Subsequent to doing a touch of work in the workplace I sat out on the back yard, watching out at the backwoods.

"There you are..." Navaar said as he strolled up next to me. He kissed the highest point of my head prior to sitting close to me.

"What's going on?" I asked, clasping his hand with mine.

"The question with that pack in the south is going crazy. I need to bring one more force and head down there myself. Ideally, I might be away for a day. That implies an IOU on that date..."

I scowled, "Okay." I got up from my seat and went higher up with Navaar to pack. At the point when he completed I pulled him near me, folding my arms over his midsection firmly. "Be protected and returned home soon."

Navaar grinned and kissed my lips delicately, "As quick as possible."

"Great, " I answered with a grin, "You actually owe me a date."

Navaar kissed me again prior to moving into his SUV. "Maya," he called out. I strolled to the driver's side and laid my hands on the window ledge.

"Better believe it?" I said cheerfully.

"I love you," Navaar murmured.

I grinned splendidly, "Navaar, I love you as well."

Navaar smiled prior to inclining his head out the window and setting a profound kiss all the rage, taking the air out of my lungs. He gave me a wink as I ventured back and watched him drive off in the distance. I took a full breath, not exactly prepared to be responsible for the pack. Fortunately Shayna was here to help while Christain and Navaar were gone. I strolled once again into the house and searched briefly prior to concluding we expected to prepare things for when they all returned. Some might be harmed and every one of them would be worn out and hungry. Shayna and I started arranging things, realizing they could be back in an hour or seven days.

The following morning I woke with an unexpected fear, similar to something didn't feel right. I strolled down the stairs to observe Shayna had a similar inclination. Unexpectedly I felt the pack interface go haywire.

"LUNA! LUNA!" somebody brought out over the connection.

"What is it?" I hollered.

"The boundary has been penetrated! We don't have a clue the number of are coming, yet with the Alpha and three contingents gone it doesn't look great."

I took a full breath, making an effort not to freeze. "Get the ladies in general and youngsters down to the packhouse dugout," I called out, utilizing the force of my Luna to ensure everybody heard it.

I remained at the entry of the dugout, helping everybody inside, stress composed on their appearances as we pondered who might assault Eclipse.

"That is everybody, " a watchman said prior to guiding me inside. We fixed the entryway shut and sat peacefully, everybody dreading for their families. Despite the fact that everybody was prepared, the kids actually required assurance. I sat, pausing my breathing as I heard clearly strides above us inside the packhouse.

"Maya..." I heard Navaar murmur in my mind.

"Navaar!" I called out, "Where could you be?"

"We just crossed once more into the region. We will be there in a moment. Where are you?" he inquired.

"I took the ladies as a whole and youngsters down to the dugout," I answered.

"Great, all of you stay safe," he answered.

I took a full breath, happy Navaar was headed to help.

"How could anybody even get in?" Jayda asked, disarray in her voice.

I shrugged, "With three brigades and the Alpha gone it probably been simpler. Fortunately, we are on the whole protected and ideally very few will be harmed in this battle."

We as a whole quieted as we heard development above us. I paused my breathing, trusting Navaar would be okay. Abruptly I felt a burning aggravation in my chest. I heaved as I multiplied over, the agony nearly as terrible as the aggravation of being dismissed.

"Luna?!" Shayna hollered as she grasped my shoulders, not exactly realizing what was going on.

I accepting a full breath as the aggravation died down.

"What was that?" Jayda asked as she and Shayna gazed at me in disarray.

"I don't know..." I answered discreetly.

Everybody panted boisterously when there was an abrupt beating on the entryway of the dugout. "It's me, Beta Christian. It's all over now, open the entryway."

I moaned in help prior to opening the entryway. He gave me a comforting grin prior to racing to his mate and youngsters.

"Where's Navaar?" I asked as everybody started recording out of the fortification.

Christian hitched his temple, "I don't know, I figured he would be first down here."

I strolled higher up and searched for him prior to letting out a compulsory shout. Lying on the floor in the conference center was my mate, wounded and grisly from his battle. I raced to him, turning him over delicately as I looked through his body.

"Navaar... Navaar wake up..." I cried, trusting he wasn't quite so gone as I suspected he was.

Chapter 22
(Final chapter)

MAYA

It had been fourteen days since the assault on our pack. From what we had accumulated, the pack that assaulted us had become irate that we generally mediated in the undertakings of different packs, evidently not understanding we possibly interceded when inquired. Overshadow had taken care of a question with them and they would rather avoid the result.

I sat at Navaar's work area with my head in my grasp, attempting to sort out some way to do all of this work that I didn't exactly comprehend. How is it that I could run a pack? Fortunately Christian had been a major assistance. I shook my head prior to leaving the workplace and strolling into our condo. I strolled into the space to observe Navaar sitting in the bed perusing a book. The one who had assaulted Navaar had gotten him unsuspecting a silver cutting edge, slicing through his skin and making it difficult to recuperate.

"How is it you become on bed rest and I need to do the entirety of the difficult work?" I asked wryly as I sat close to him on the bed.

Navaar grinned prior to pulling me in for a kiss. "Since you weren't nearly cut down the middle," he answered.

I ran my give over his chest, feeling the scar that went from his left shoulder down to the center of his right ribcage. Navaar shuddered at the touch and snarled profoundly, "Cautious, Luna. Or then again I'll need to take myself off bed rest. Fourteen days without you is excessively long."

I chuckled prior to kissing his cheek and jumping off the bed. "Well pick up the pace and improve then, at that point."

Navaar reclined against the headboard, "I'm chipping away at it."

I left the room, wanting to be better so I could share my news. I had discovered last week that I was pregnant and had been needing to tell him, yet never appeared to track down the right second I needed it to be huge and exceptional yet I had no clue about what to do.

NAVAAR

That evening I looked as Maya strolled around the room prior to strolling into the storeroom to change.

"Hello! Would you be able to snatch my scratch pad from the cabinet of my side table and read off my daily agenda for later?" she hollered.

I murmured prior to hanging over to her side of the bed and hauling her scratch pad out of the cabinet.

"OK... One: Finish entrance desk work for Kline's. Two: Set up providing food for pack supper. Three: Tell Navaar I'm pr-"

I gazed upward with shock to see Maya remaining close to the bed happily, "Please accept my apologies, I didn't hear that final remaining one."

I peered down at the third thing on her rundown, wrote in her penmanship. "Three: Tell Navaar I'm pregnant..." I murmured.

Maya sat on the bed next to me and grasped my hand, "Don't be vexed... I just-"

I gobbled my face up to hers, "Steamed?" I took her face in my grasp, "Maya, this is the most astounding thing of all time. Maya, we will have a little guy!"

Maya grinned as tears filled her eyes, "We will have a puppy!"

I kissed her hotly, needing her to realize exactly the amount I adored her right now.

"Maya, I love you," I said as I measured her face in my grasp.

"I love you more," Maya said prior to kissing my lips. She pulled back and set down in the bed, our bodies weaving as we held each other close.

A half year after the fact

MAYA

"Navaar... Navaar wake up..." I said discreetly as I shook
him.

"Mmmmm," he protested prior to turning over.

"Navaar, I-well.."

Navaar immediately sat up, "Maya, what's going on?"

"The child, it's coming," I answered, keeping my eyes shut
tight with the expectation that it would make the
compressions disappear.

Navaar leaped up and got dressed prior to assisting me with
trip of bed and getting my sack. He strolled me to the pack
clinical structure, shutting down now and again for a major
withdrawal.

"Well," the attendant said cheerfully, "This child is coming
without a doubt. We should get you set up and meet this
little puppy!"

I strained as one more influx of compressions hit, the agony getting further with every one.

Following a two hours and a few dangers focused on Navaar, our sweet young lady at long last came.

Lydia Marie was conceived and I cried as I held her in my arms.

"I'm so glad for you, angel," Navaar murmured as he put a kiss on my temple.

"You're not frustrated that it's anything but a kid?" I inquired.

Navaar shook his head, "She will be the greatest, baddest, champion Alpha in this pack. Her daddy will ensure that."

I grinned prior to peering down at our child young lady, "Great since she's totally awesome."

As I laid in my clinic bed I grinned as I took a gander at Lydia and Navaar both dozing calmly. I contemplated how far we had come. Right now I had all that I had ever longed for. A home, a family, and love.

Please review and comment

THANK YOU